What Killed Doctor K.?

BARBARA KOTLER

What Killed Doctor K.?
© Copyright 2015, Barbara Kotler

ISBN 978-0-9908871-0-2

IndieReader Publishing Services
Montclair, New Jersey

*To my loving husband
who is the most
caring person I know.*

Acknowledgements

I wish to thank my editor Barbara Cronie for her
support and encouragement. She is the best!

I also want to thank the Writers Colony
for their critiques of my writing that
certainly helped make me a better writer.

Preface

Society will never be the same as when things in the medical world were less complicated and not controlled by the policies of corporate health care, sometimes doing more harm than good. Of course, most everything was more simplistic and easier in the '60s when Dr. K. chose to begin the difficult job of caregiver to humanity. This is a fictional story, not a mystery, based on a true story of that caregiver as seen through the eyes of Dr. K's wife. But it tells the tale of all who want to heal.

Dr. K. had a lifetime of adventures and experience. As a physician in the United States Air Force during the Vietnam War, as an occupational doctor in industry, and in his own private practice, his story is compelling. He exemplifies all the young, eager, idealistic docs who were under the impression, when they received their MD degrees, they actually could save patients in their small part of the world and do it their way.

This novel is an informative history and passionate glimpse of the practice of medicine as it used to be. It chronicles what it takes to become a physician, with all the rewards and all the stress. It is an insider's personal accounting of what most of us are unaware of and could never imagine. It may stun you, but perhaps not surprise you.

Introduction

The oppressively hot, humid summer season had already begun, but on that particular day, my heart was stone cold. My dear soul mate had quietly passed from this world and an aching, deep sadness had washed over me. I stood over the plain, pine box that was his coffin with my private thoughts, which were screaming at me that he did not have to leave this way. He should not have left at all.

The people at the gravesite were just a blur to me, and it's hard to remember what words of sympathy they offered. I was like a robot, shaking hands and acknowledging everyone, almost in an out-of-body state. Soon salty tears fell nonstop down my cheeks and puddled on the top of my blouse.

Gloomy, grey clouds started rolling in, gripping me with fear that a rainstorm was on its way. At the same time, I wished it would pour, as if somehow the rain could wash away this sorrowful scene.

I surrendered to the pain, as I watched shovelful after shovelful of rich, brown earth being thrown into the hole, surrounding the coffin, sheltering his body.

His body was short in stature, but had the heart of a giant. He had resembled an old sea captain, with a coarse, authoritative voice as if he were directing a ship's crew. He had a thick, full head of dirty blonde hair. Just a bit of grey sparkled in his sideburns as well as in his blonde mustache, and it seemed to compliment his tan, ruddy complexion. Bushy, yellow, rather unkempt eyebrows framed laughing hazel eyes that looked as if they had seen too much of life. Thin laugh lines and deep wrinkles gave him that weathered look, but did not detract from his handsome face. The most notable thing about his good looks was his shaped-to-perfection nose. His posture was always straight and proud. He had a very strong presence.

In the coffin, he appeared so frail and small. His laughing face had turned still and grim.

"Come back, come back!" I shouted to myself. "Please don't leave!"

But he was gone, taking with him all the struggles and injustices of his life and career, but leaving all the love and enduring respect behind.

Chapter 1

It had been ages since I was in Philadelphia, and it felt good walking down Chestnut Street, located in the center of the city. It seemed so different than I remembered. Of course nothing stays the same, so why should time have stopped on Chestnut Street? My memory cruised back to 1960 when I wouldn't be seen walking on any city street without being dressed up in high heels and wearing my spotless, white gloves. I'm sure glad we've come a long way from that scene.

A walk down Chestnut was always a visual treat then, with an array of smart outfits parading up and down the grey, uneven, cobblestoned sidewalks. A short stroll across Broad Street brought me to Wanamaker Department Store, where I had spent hours browsing and dreaming as a poor medical student's wife. Wanamaker's, it seemed, had not changed. The store was crowded and bustling. On the first floor the familiar, bronze, twelve-foot-high eagle stood watch like a store security guard over three floors of a brass-bannistered merchandise market.

I couldn't help strolling over to the infamous eagle and hoped no one was noticing me. I petted its smooth, cold, bronze side. I suspect there were thousands before me who participated in that ritual, and there would be many more after me. The eagle was at the center of the universe, at the crossroads of the city, where people met and left, where they fought and made up, and sometimes parted forever. "Meet me at the eagle" was a popular Philly phrase. Well, here I was, many years later, feeling very much at home with the magic eagle.

I sat under the eagle, and my mind drifted back to the days of being very young in Philadelphia. My husband Ben was attending Jefferson Medical College, and I was glad he was going to school in that city. It had so much to offer. Beyond all the cultural sites, there were those wonderful greasy steak sandwiches served with tons of onions and generic cheese and overstuffed hoagies with lots of hot peppers and everything else but the kitchen sink. We took weekend breaks to tootle around the city with nothing but our dreams to keep us struggling forward.

I taught school to keep us in food and clothing and Ben joined the United States Air Force, as a second lieutenant under the Berry Plan, to keep a roof over our heads and help with tuition. The Berry Plan was quite a plan. The United States Air Force paid for a medical student's schooling in exchange for several years of service. It certainly worked for us! We scrounged tickets to the concerts at the Academy of Music from a friend who was music major at a local college and ran to the museums whenever there was a free exhibition. On Sundays, we very often spent the entire day in bed, languishing between making love and reading the Sunday papers. We didn't know it then, but we were in heaven.

Our stay in heaven was short-lived. The trials and tribulations of my husband attending medical school were quite overwhelming, and especially so, because we were still so young. Actually, on the flip side, there were times when my youth carried me through some experiences that I could never have handled as a grown woman.

While husband Ben was in school, we lived in an old, age-worn hotel that had been converted into tired rental apartments. The lobby was a sanctuary to many homeless people. There was no one to chase them from their private haven from the cold or heat and the ever present danger of the not-to-be trusted streets in a big city. It was amazing, though, how much respect they had for the tired, white-coated doctors who staggered home each evening from their little bit of hell at the hospital. There was always a hello to greet the docs and many thankful hands that reached out to shake the hands of the doctors who had probably treated them sometime during the week.

What was not so great were the roaches that inhabited just about every square inch of living space in our dilapidated apartment. Even though I became a cleaning nut, it was not enough to keep them away. The only way, I soon discovered, to be able to cook and serve a meal without them hanging out with me, was to stack some bread in a corner for diversion. While they feasted on old Wonder Bread, I could scurry around just as fast as they did and finish my job. The worst part was when they discovered our bedroom and wanted to share our bed. If the lights were on, they would stay hidden, and so we learned to sleep with a bright, glaring lamp near our bed that acted like a cross, warding off vampires.

I so remember the stories that Ben brought home from the hospital. It seems like yesterday when he told me, with the most satisfied, gentle smile that I had ever seen, of an episode where he involuntarily delivered a baby. It happened as he was waiting for an elevator in the hospital. When the doors opened, he was confronted with a woman on a gurney, her legs open wide, facing him and getting ready to deliver her baby. Having no option, he held his hands out and received the precious little one. The attendant who was in back of the gurney had no room to step forward and assist, but with the instruments he removed from his pocket, Ben was able to cut and clamp the umbilical cord. As Ben was relating the story to me, he had tears in his eyes, and I knew for sure that this man was going to make a special physician. He cared. Little did he realize then, that given the future of medicine, he was on a collision course when "caring" would crash with greed and deception.

One of the most memorable nights I experienced during this time was the night at DBI (Dead Body Institute). That building housed all the dead bodies the medical students worked on to learn all they could about the human body. It was beyond imagination to think of these students, knives in hand, cutting up bodies on an information quest, much like cutting up frogs in a biology class. They handled the organs as an autopsy, all for the sake of learning and discovery. Several of them succumbed to turning green and throwing up. Most, like Ben, just became hardened robots doing what the instructor wanted. My friend and I were fascinated by all the stories that Ben and his fellow students told of the inhabitants of DBI. We heard all the gruesome stories but begged to be taken up to see the cadavers that the students were working on.

It was finally arranged, and one night my friend, her boyfriend, and Ben and I were let into the building by a bribed guard. I felt like I was in a class B horror film when we entered the room where the bodies were. The smell of formaldehyde permeated the room and made me gag. About thirty bodies were laid out on white granite tables with white sheets covering them, and I half expected them to all rise, throw off their sheets, and chase after us. I was beginning to feel very cold, and every hair on my arms was spiked. In all actuality, I had never seen a real dead body and it totally spooked me. Ben pulled the sheet from one of the corpses that he was assigned to and I became quite interested. It was a man who had died of lung cancer from smoking, and the dried bloody flaps of his chest were cut and thrown open. His X-ray was up on a screen, and when it was lighted, I could see that on one side of his lungs there were perfectly lined up ribs, but on the other side there was just one large black blob. That sight burned a spot in my brain till this day.

When we left the building and walked out into the street, I headed toward a storm drain. I took my pack of Marlboro cigarettes and threw them into the drain. "If I have to die, I am not going to die of lung cancer from smoking," I announced. I never smoked after that night.

I must say that I was in awe of these young men who strived to be physicians and struggled each day trying to learn or memorize the volumes of material that would lay the foundation of their knowledge and allow them to attempt to heal the sick. It was mind-stretching. They were the best and the brightest, brought together to develop skills and judgment to help people in need.

Sometimes I read and studied along with Ben and his friends. I discovered a new, strange, spiritual side to myself as I uncovered all the medical mysteries of the makeup of the human body. It is nothing short of a miracle. The plan and creation of the body cannot possibly be mere happenstance. The design is so intricate, perfect, and exact. This scientific awakening just stimulated another awakening in me. It cemented my belief in a higher power that surely is the architect of this incredible creation. And it gave me a new set of eyes to appreciate these future caretakers of man.

At the time, neither Ben nor I had enough appreciation for what a wonderful medical school Jefferson was. It seemed the focus of the curriculum was on the whole person in evaluating disease. This was the catalyst that allowed many of the graduating doctors, including Ben, to practice good diagnostic medicine. I know that a complete physical examination was standard in his practice, and preventive medicine was the key to his patients' good health. Of course, it was not until the '90s that this was a totally accepted philosophy. So, for a while, it was hard to convince patients of the need to actually guard their health before they became sick. It seemed easier for them to read about the newest medicine in *Readers Digest* (sometimes before the doctor knew about it) and demand that they be given a prescription for what ailed them.

What was not wonderful about the school was some of the professors. One in particular must have been a bit crazy. It was

June, 1961, the last week of school for the graduating seniors, and some of them still had a final exam to complete. The guys studying at our apartment were in a total frenzy after a particular professor told them that if they received any mark on the exam lower than seventy-five, they would not be graduating. No one could believe it. Four years of hell and one test mark was going to determine their future. The unfairness of it all made me edgy, but all the docs came through, and the class graduated as a whole. What a graduation day that was! We partied well into the night. The graduates had all survived unearned suffering only to emerge as bright new spirits ready to heal the world.

Chapter 2

Our real-life adventure started after graduation. Before that, it was just a dress rehearsal. Ben had three years committed to the United States Air Force and off we drove to our new home at Lackland Air Force Base in San Antonio, Texas. We felt this was a real privilege for Ben to be doing an internship at Lackland Hospital. This base was very active at that time, and most new recruits did their basic training there. He was an officer (second lieutenant) and so our expectations were high. After all, being an officer in the USAF was not too shabby. Of course the world situation was not settled in the early '60s, and all eyes were on the country of Vietnam, half a world away, and we were thankful to be exactly where we were.

The new interns were thrown right into their assignments. The schedules were grueling. The docs worked two nights in a row and then had one off. It seemed to me they all walked around looking like zombies, and I could not figure out how beneficial that would be to patients. But I learned that this was the norm. They mostly took care of the young recruits and also worked in the clinics taking care of military dependents. They rotated through every department to become proficient in each phase of medicine. Luck was not on Ben's side, though. Every new intern had an assigned partner who completed and reported on patient charts with their partner. Unfortunately, Ben's partner never showed up to fill out charts, so he was stuck with all the extra work. I hardly ever saw him because he was actually doing the work of two people. He was not happy. The intern was discharged from the service, which did not help Ben; he still had to do the work of two. So we could do nothing but joke about it and say that he learned twice as much.

One night Ben came home looking upset. A young recruit had gone AWOL, and that day the military police found his body in the desert around the air base. The vultures had eaten most of his face away, and being in charge of the team that had to claim and bag the body, Ben was rattled. The worst part was when the parents came to identify the young man, and Ben then had the job of consoling the family.

Medicine as a science then took on a different character. It became an art, the art of compassion. "I feel your pain," he told them. And he truly did for weeks after they had taken their son home.

About a month later, one of the recruits was brought into the emergency room on Ben's shift. He complained of incredible fatigue and severe pain. He was completely dehydrated and near death. Along with a complete physical examination where nothing could be found, a history was taken. The recruit told of having to carry around a huge fifty-pound rock to every activity, including running ten miles, as a punishment for some infraction of the rules. He did this every day for three days in ninety-five degree weather. Apparently this was not considered cruel or unusual punishment. The recruit was hospitalized, but be assured that, after the doctors had a conference on this case, no more rocks were being lugged around that air base.

Most of his internship was tough; Ben lost weight and didn't sleep much. Internship was all about learning and getting experience. It exposed the doctors to a smattering of all the departments of medicine and most medical problems. We hardly ever saw each other, but it was also the year our first child was born, which was just joyful.

The night of his arrival was a comedy. Ben had been on duty for two shifts, equal to almost forty-eight hours with no sleep. When he came home, he decided to take a sleeping pill so he could fall asleep quickly and get some real rest. Of course, as life would have it, he had just about fallen asleep when my water broke, and I ran into the bedroom shouting and crying in excitement. My husband sat straight up in bed and said, "What's happening?"

"My water broke!"

"Oh my God!" he shouted. "Go stand in the shower."

I ran into the bathroom, and after about ten minutes of standing in the bathtub when he did not appear, I screamed for him to come.

He quickly arrived at the door, looked at me standing in the tub, and yelled, "What the hell are you doing standing in the bathtub?"

"You told me to," I shouted back. I burst into tears and cried until he helped me out and took me to the hospital where, after eighteen hours of labor (with my doctor, Hal Morgan, reading the Sunday newspaper comic strips while leaning on my belly), our precious little boy Scott was born. This new little life lifted us up and so balanced our existence.

When I later asked Ben why he told me to stand in the tub, he said that, coming from a deep sleep, "all I could think of was that when your water broke it would have ruined the rug."

We met many interesting people at the air base. Air Force generals and astronauts would commonly show up in the medical department, and Ben would come home with fascinating stories. He was part of the team in charge of several aspects of the astronauts' examinations. He was able to go to Brooks Air Force Base and participate in their survival school. He loved it!

It was an incredibly diverse internship and being on an Air Force base stimulated his love of the service and flying. He was even seriously considering a service career at that point.

Air Force people share an intense comradeship. Because their families are at a distance, their neighbors and friends become their families, making it quite comforting. My neighbor Pam was from England and was married to Bill, the PR officer of the base hospital. She had three children and was able to give me all the good tips about babies. She was better than Dr. Spock. We became close, and so when her mother-in-law came for a visit, we were welcomed over to have dinner and meet Mom. It seemed that Mom had a penchant for reading tarot cards, and after dinner she asked me if I would like her to read for me. I agreed and it was more than fascinating. I learned some interesting things, including my husband and I would soon be taking a trip halfway around the world. I thought that was a bit much and totally discounted her prediction. I did not know, at that point in my young life, if I believed all she told me from the cards. I later learned she could not have been more on target.

Graduation Day, 1962, was one happy day. A year of learning, practice, and sweat had come to an end, and now this group of young doctors would be choosing their specialty and be off to see the world. I remember sitting in the front row with the other over-the-top-proud wives.

I felt scared but emotionally high as we all listened to the base commander's speech. "Just remember," he said, "you are officers first, doctors second, and husbands third."

We all looked at each other, and one of the girls said, in a voice that was a tad too loud, "Hell no, they are husbands first, doctors second, and officers third."

The commander looked like he had just swallowed a toad but managed to finish his address, and as soon as it was over, we all escaped quickly to the refreshment table for a glass of wine punch. Internship was over, and now all we had to do was wait for the new assignments to come in the next week. Ben received his captain's rank and was pleased. It was spring, a time of new beginnings, and we were anxious about ours.

The week after graduation seemed to last forever while we waited for Ben's next assignment. Finally the letter came assigning him to Japan for two years. He was the only one in his class to be sent out of the country. I thought that they were kidding. I couldn't separate from him for two years. The option was that I did not have to. I could go with him if he signed up for another year. Well, that was a no brainer. He would sign and I would go. Now we had to figure a way to break the news to our families. This was before computers or we might have just e-mailed them, but instead we called and had to listen to responses that were not pretty. Our parents wanted to know how we could leave them and couldn't we tell the Air Force that we needed a stateside assignment? After the telephone barrage, we hung up and danced around the house realizing we were being given a great opportunity to go to a foreign country with all expenses paid for by the US government.

We went back to New Jersey in the fall and made the rounds among all our friends and relatives to show off our five-month-old little boy. We also had a chance to tell everyone that I was over three months pregnant. Of course, with that news, our parents were even more upset, but before long we were on our way to San Francisco to board an Air Force plane that would take us halfway round the world.

Chapter 3

Our cross-country flight was not too bad, but when we connected to the air base where our plane waited for the journey to Japan, we were stunned. We were told that the flight would take twenty-six hours on a prop plane, and we needed to head to the other side of the airport to catch our plane, which was scheduled to leave at any moment. We ran like hell!

Our hands were filled with all kinds of baby paraphernalia, plus baby, and we were running as fast as we could to catch our plane. And then the inevitable happened. I felt a loose, warm liquid run down my skirt from the baby. It had some consistency, so it did not drop to the floor and it did not smell very good. The baby started to howl. I stopped, not knowing what in the world I should do. Did I dare pause to change a diaper and risk missing the plane? Ben saw the predicament and shouted he would run ahead to tell them to hold the plane. All I wanted to do was cry.

Then my angel appeared. She was an older, good-looking, red-haired woman who whisked Scott out of my arms and told me to follow her as she knew where the ladies' room was. In there—I could hardly believe it—she laid her clean, starched, Burberry raincoat on the disgusting floor (this was before baby changers) and proceeded to clean and change the screaming child with calm and patience. Apparently she had done this drill before. She said she would hold Scott as we ran to the plane. The plane had waited for us, and we climbed aboard. She introduced herself as Rita and also introduced her husband Carl and volunteered to hold the baby on her lap so we could settle back in our seats. Carl was a printer for *Stars and Stripes*, the Armed Forces newspaper, and they had taken this trip before with children. My angel took turns holding the baby all through the grueling twenty-six-hour flight and promised to keep in touch when we set down at Yokota Air Base. We absolutely did keep in touch, and Rita and Carl became wonderful friends and surrogate grandparents while we were overseas.

A lovely couple, Jane and Henry, who were our sponsors, met

us at the plane. They were very excited and told us they were whisking us away to have our first Japanese meal of our tour. We tried to be polite and agreed to go, but all I wanted to do was shower and sleep. It had been a long, challenging journey, and trying to entertain a six-month-old ball of energy and keep awake was the biggest challenge. Of course, being pregnant did not help because through it all, a feeling of sickness made me uncomfortable.

By the time we arrived at the restaurant, I felt more like dying than eating, but our sponsors were anxious to be the first ones to introduce us to sushi, wasabi, seaweed, and green tea. Looking at all that raw fish gave me the shivers. I have grown to love all these things, but at the time, all I wanted to do was throw up. I struggled through the meal being eternally grateful that my sweet baby slept the whole time. When we arrived at our motel, I just wanted to crash and sleep forever. But to my annoyance that was not on the agenda. When I gazed out the window, which looked onto the front of the air base gate, I saw about one hundred Japanese men walking in front of the gate with huge signs reading "Yankee go home." Were they kidding? That's all I wanted to do at that moment. I had traveled all these miles just to see these signs? America had won the war, completely built up this country, and now they wanted us to go home? The tears burst forth like water from a broken dyke. I wanted my mom, my dad, my friends, my hometown, and my country, and I was sure I would not like it there one single bit. I cried all night.

The next morning, bright and early, our enthusiastic sponsors appeared to take us to breakfast and show us around the base. I was grateful we ate at the Officers Club, hereafter referred to as the O Club. No sushi for breakfast. I was so happy. We toured everywhere on the base and then went to look at housing. There were no vacancies on the air base so we went looking for a small house on "the economy," as those houses off the base were called. It was very discouraging. The small houses were called paddy houses because they were located in an area surrounded by paddy fields where rice was grown. We did find one, though, that was halfway acceptable. Weathered, foggy plastic covered all the windows. Of course, there was no central heat, just a small, old, black propane heater, looking ugly and sitting smack in the middle of the living room. This was meant to heat the whole house. The kitchen was so tiny that, being pregnant as I was, when I walked into the kitchen, the only way I could get out was to back out! The bathroom was bigger than the kitchen, with a huge, Japanese-style, sunken tub. Three people could sit in this tub at the same time with extra room. However, the tub was three long steps down. The steps seemed definitely problematic, but we needed to get settled so we rented it. Ah... I can still see myself in my wonderful tub, soaking for hours just like most of the people traditionally did in Japan. Our belongings came in three days, so at the end of the week we were moved in.

Ben started in the flight surgeon's office the next day. While I unpacked and put everything away, I realized how terribly lonely I was. All I had was a six-month-old to babble to all day. I loved his gurgles back to me, but it was not enough to sustain my sanity. We were in the middle of a Japanese village surrounded by Japanese people, and I could not speak their language. It was not too promising. When Ben came home one night and announced he would be gone for several days on his first flying mission, I was in a panic. The first night alone I kept hearing noises outside my window, and by the second night, I became totally fearful. When I heard someone knocking on my door, I grabbed Scott and froze in terror. There were no telephones in these paddy houses and I just did not know what to do.

Then I heard a soft, singsong voice say, "Hi, it's me, your neighbor Dawn."

I joyfully flung open the door and there stood a sight to behold, a very handsome woman with an embracing smile on her face. In one hand she was holding a pitcher of martinis and, in the other, a whole Sara Lee cheesecake.

"My husband left on the same flight as yours, and I thought you might need some company," she said.

I could not believe that standing in front of me was a wonderful, friendly neighbor holding martinis and cheesecake too. Wow! This was too good to be true. I later learned that this was what the service was all about. This was the exceptional caring that was the glue that kept the wives of servicemen together like family. Needless to say, we polished off the entire pitcher of gin and then the both of us devoured that creamy cheese delight. Dear Dawn was to become my lifelong friend.

Living in the paddies turned out to be quite a challenge, especially in the damp, dingy winter. The Air Force had issued safety rules mostly about the outdated propane heaters. We were not allowed to have them on during the night for obvious reasons. So, if anyone saw how we dressed to sleep, they would have cracked up. The baby had three layers past his diaper and pj's, topped off with a hooded snowsuit and gloves. Ben and I layered cotton, thermal underwear, wool sweaters, pants, and down ski jackets. Once in bed we could not move, and forget about going to the bathroom. Sex was out of the question; changing a diaper was an hour job. And we did this for three months!

One morning when I went to start up the heater, it would not start. When we went outside to check the propane tank, we saw a siphon lying on the ground. Someone had stolen all our propane during the night. Apparently this was a common activity, and we learned that we had to put a lock on the tank. Actually we had to put a lock on nearly everything of value as there seemed to be an epidemic of theft. Thank goodness, we finally moved onto the base, where there was steam heat and a telephone. We had a big kitchen, living room, dining room, two bedrooms, and bath. There was even a good-sized yard. Now, this was good living. To make it even better, we hired a babysitter for what amounted to two dollars and seventy-five cents a week. We did this just in time for our precious baby number two to enter this world through the Japanese connection.

On that particular day, I had traveled off the base in my little ten-year-old secondhand Renault. This car was just suited to Japanese roads, which were two-lane gravel highways with benjo ditches on either side. The ditches were used as sewers and were convenient if you had to relieve yourself while driving (which Japanese men had no problem doing). Also, ditches made sure that no one would drive on the shoulder of the road for any reason. If you had a problem you were sheer out of luck.

I was off to have my hair done at the local Japanese beauty salon. I was almost finished under the dryer, with those huge round curlers in my hair, when I felt that I was sitting in a puddle of water. I looked at my skirt and saw it was soaked. I realized my water had broken and shouted for the girls to get me out of the chair and get the curlers out of my hair. They scurried around to make me look good and hastened me out of the salon. No way was there going to be a birth at their salon on their watch.

As I stood on the sidewalk, I knew I had to get in my car and drive myself to the hospital at another air base, where my doctor was. There were no telephones to use and, of course, no cell phones. Yes, indeed, there was no other way but to get on the highway and drive twenty minutes to the hospital if I wanted this baby delivered. What a ride it was! Every time I had a contraction I stopped dead in the middle of the road and let the contraction and pain pass. Cars backed up behind me and did not have a choice. They could not pass and laid on their horns. It did not rattle me. I talked back to them through the rearview mirror and out of the open window.

"Sorry, guys, I'm having a baby and cannot do anything about this," I yelled. They did not understand a thing I was saying. So each contraction was another stop the rest of the way. The cars in back of me were a mile long by the time I turned into the hospital driveway, and as each one passed, the driver gave me the finger. Funny how they all seemed to understand that!

Fifteen minutes after arriving, I was shaved and prepped and sweet Michael made his appearance. It was moments later that his dad arrived for the event. And I never really found out how he knew to show up at that exact time. Some things you chalk up to serendipity. Our anniversary was the day after Michael's birth, and although no flowers were allowed in my room, Daddy smuggled in a long-stemmed, velvety red rose — life was good.

It was 1963 and the Vietnam War was in full force at that time. Ben had the responsibility of not only the dependents of the squad he was assigned to but the whole squad of fliers who rotated through Vietnam in the cockpit of their fighter jets. They were jet jockeys who knew their lives were on the line every time they took off from Yokota Air Force Base. The job colored their health, attitude, sanity, and all aspects of their family life. They were very young men who became hardened to the war's atrocities and wore masks of cockiness to conceal their fear. So, in addition to practicing general medicine, the doctors who tended to these warriors needed to be trauma docs, psychiatrists, and counselors. They needed to be close to the families for support, as everyone grappled with patriotism and the horrific situation they were in. The doctor's wife had to know every wife in the squadron and be open to being called upon for any little problem.

On one occasion, one of the wives appeared at my door at two in the morning while Ben was away, and I found myself in the position of being mother confessor and counselor to her. I was only twenty-five years old but did myself proud when I talked her out of committing suicide. She had followed her husband off the base to a Japanese girl's house, peered in the window, and saw them having sex. She was devastated, but said she still loved her husband and did not know what to do. In my inexperienced but logical way I told her to confront her husband and give him a choice. Either he stop seeing this girl and they go to counseling, or she would go to his commander and tell him the story. If it got to his commander, he would most likely be disciplined and lose flying pay, which would go on his record. The pilot made the right decision. They stayed together, got counseling, and I was feeling like I could take on anything in our Air Force experience.

Of course, I really was not prepared for what happened to our neighbor a few months later.

Whenever a plane was shot down or lost in flight, a team comprised of a flight surgeon, chaplain, and commander was sent out to bring the awful news to the wife or family. On this particular spring night, we had opened the windows after a rain shower to bring in the evening's fresh scent. We fell into bed and were almost asleep when the phone rang ordering Ben to join the team being sent out on a condolence call to one of the houses on the base. After he left, I lay in bed enjoying the smells of grass, earth, and rain from the open window. I peered out of the window to gaze at a muddy, black sky when I saw Ben, the Catholic chaplain, and squadron commander on the porch of my neighbor. I suspected in an instant what they were doing. When the porch light went on and I heard a chilling, piercing scream, I knew for sure. This should not be happening to the nice young couple and new baby next door. The team disappeared inside and I lay there sobbing and cursing the war and the governments that created it.

Shortly afterward, Ben was off again on a distant three-week assignment. It was while he was gone that I received a very weird phone call. The phone rang one night quite late, and when I answered it, a woman was babbling away, half-laughing and half-crying with excitement. She asked if she had reached the home of Dr. Kazinski. I hesitated because professionally he was called Dr. K. When I said "yes," she identified herself as Betty and started on her tirade. I couldn't understand exactly what she was saying because she talked so fast, but it was something about knowing Ben and his family. She wanted to come right over, but when I told her that Ben was not home and wouldn't be for another week, she simmered down and accepted instead an invitation for coffee upon his return. We set up a night and time. I felt that I had just traveled through a wind tunnel, and upon hanging up the phone, I had to ask myself what had just happened and why in the world had I invited this stranger to my home for coffee. Oh, she seemed nice enough, but what was I thinking?

I was so happy when Ben returned that I almost forgot it was the same day that I had invited this woman, who supposedly knew his family, to come over. He did not put any pieces together from the brief conversation I related to him. I had just set the table for our mystery guest, including a cake that I whipped up, when the doorbell rang announcing our visitor, or should I say visitors: Betty and her husband John. Well, she sailed through our front door and threw her arms around me in a smothering hug, taking my breath away. In an instant, I connected to her warmth and vivacious personality.

"Oh my God, we are so happy to have found you," she declared. We can't believe you're here! We are halfway round the world and so are you. Isn't that amazing?" After she planted a long kiss on Ben and introduced her husband, she proceeded to tell us, over several cups of coffee, who she was and the unbelievable story of how she found us.

"You see," she explained, "I am the sister of Julie, the nurse who tended Ben's mother Claire when Ben's sister Susan was born. We all became friendly, and I even dated Alan, Claire's brother. Those friendships were maintained for years, and I continued to write Alan after he married and moved to London, England."

It seems that Betty's husband was a navy man, but when he retired, he took a position with Pratt Whitney and was sent to Japan to consult on the jet engine manufactured by Pratt Whitney and used by the Air Force in the Vietnam War. He was processed through the medical department at Yokota Air Base for his physical exam, and when he arrived home afterward, he related to Betty that his exam was the best he ever had. At the time Betty was writing to her friend Alan in London and included John's remarks about his exam in the letter. When Alan wrote back, he commented he was glad John was pleased with the medical care he received and added that he believed his young nephew had been assigned to an air base in Japan, and if they ever came across him, his name was Ben.

As Betty read the letter to John, he interrupted, "That's him, that's him! Ben was the name of the doc who gave me my exam."

That is what prompted the weird call and the crazy visit. Of course, after hearing her story, it became clear we felt connected and happy to have a loving extended family in Japan. To know Betty was to love her, and John was clearly the nicest man ever! Betty knew just about everyone on the planet, and I always told people what a serious Catholic she was. No matter what airport she flew into, a priest would meet her and take care of her. It was way over the top. They were our adopted family and that relationship was for all time.

Sometimes the pilots got a bit rambunctious. When a few of them landed in Okinawa for some rest and relaxation, they headed for the O Club, where the drinks in those days were twenty-five cents. They had a bag full of piranha which they dumped into the exotic fish tank that ran the length of the ten-foot-long bar. The half-sloshed pilots drank the night away while watching all the fish disappear and the evil, little piranha take over the tank! That was just one of the pranks I heard about. There were lots of crazy stories, most of them about the horrors taking place in Vietnam.

When we went overseas, we were very pro-war because of all the political reasoning that we were subjected to. As we heard more and more stories from the pilots and saw how people were reacting in the States—picketing and protesting against the war—we began to wonder what the hell we were involved in and why all our talented young people were being subjected to this torture. It was a war fought like no other. At any given time, our troops might not know who the enemy was. Friendly women and adorable children were used to deliver bombs, and Vietnam soldiers switched sides if their friends or relatives were on the enemy side.

Ben was flying in and out of Vietnam in planes that delivered medical supplies and brought the wounded back to the air base. The planes were routinely shot at, but I did not know any of this until we were stateside, which was probably a good thing.

One of the pilots, who came to the flight surgeon's side of the clinic for a flying personnel complete physical exam, flew fighter jets in and out of Vietnam. His name was Major Ripgard, but they called him Rip. After his exam was completed, he and Ben had an interesting chat about airplanes and flying. When Ben showed up on the flight line two weeks later for a flight to Clark Air Force Base in the Philippines (where he had been ordered to go by his commander to get a briefing on a top secret mission), he saw Rip waiting by the T33 jet he was to board. Rip told Ben that he was the pilot assigned to take him to the Philippines in one of the jets. Ben was excited and suited up to fly with flight suit, helmet, and oxygen. They flew off, and Ben was given a map and told that it was his job to direct Rip on longitude and latitude on the way to their destination. This came as a shock and completely stumped Ben because he did not know a thing about reading those types of maps. As he was trying to comply, Rip suddenly flew the jet upside down. Ben let out a whoop and thought he was going to throw up and die, in that order. He yelled at Rip to right the plane, but the pilot could not hear him, partially due to the rush of wind in the cockpit and partially because Rip was overcome with laughter.

When the plane finally leveled out right side up, Ben turned on the mike to the front and shouted, "What the hell were you doing?"

Rip replied between his fits of laughter, "Well, doc, I was just getting even for that rectal exam you punished me with a few weeks ago."

Rip and Ben remained friends for many, many years.

In between flights Ben was busy in the clinic on the base. The clinics were medicine at its finest. In those days, there was no push to see a certain number of patients each day. Preventive medicine was promoted, while pilots were given time and attention and all their needs taken care of. The Air Force doctors were very well-respected on the base which made their lives easier.

It was easy for the patients as well. All their medical needs were met, with the only hassle being a slightly long wait in the emergency room. They could return to see the same doctor if they wished. An Air Force doctor could not be sued; everything was arbitrated so they did not have to worry about that. Ben totally enjoyed this practice of medicine and even tried to pattern his own private practice to this style of medicine years later.

There were a lot of perks to compensate for being away from home and living in a stressful environment. Prices in Japan were comparatively cheap, and we were able to schedule a seamstress to come to the house and sew for about two dollars a week. She made me some beautiful outfits from the gorgeous brocades and colorful silks available in the Orient. Amazingly, the patterns she made to my measurements were cut out of brown paper bags. They were the latest designs from fashion magazines, and I felt like a princess!

We hired an adorable, little, crinkly-skinned old man named Miki-san to come every Saturday and wash our cars, also for a meager price. He loved our oldest son Scott and after he finished his job (which took about an hour), he stayed to play with Scott for several more hours. Miki-san spoke a good amount of English, and one day I invited him to join us for a cup of tea. He was delighted and kept bowing to us as a sign of deep respect. We engaged him in conversation and he shared his story.

"You were a kamikaze?" I probed. His story was fascinating. He had been in the Japanese Air Force and told us that he was engaged and about to be married to his childhood love. A notice had come inviting him to join the elite kamikaze and his family was very proud, urging him to join. He was being given the chance to be a hero. So he joined and immediately began to train, leaving his sweetheart and parents behind.

"You left your loved ones behind and were happy and proud to commit suicide?" I asked in disbelief. I was too young to fathom the whole concept of what he was telling us. To me, life was too precious to sacrifice in such a way.

He went on with his story and I was in awe. It seems he was trained well and due to go on a mission on a certain day. Unbelievably, that day was the day the war ended, and his flight was canceled. The war was over and he was sent home to his village. He arrived home in disgrace. He did not fulfill his destiny of death and could no longer be respected. His parents and fiancé would not talk to him, so he ultimately moved from his home to a town near the air base where he could make a living. I was very moved by his story, and when he left, I could not help but give Miki-san a hug and tell him I was glad he was alive. He was at our house just about every weekend for three years playing with our son in the front yard. By the sounds of the laughter, I could tell he brought sheer happiness and delight to little Scott, who adored him.

There was another encounter I vividly recall. On this particular evening, my babysitter Hodekai was preparing to say goodnight and catch a bus home. Ben was away for the week and she offered to stay at night to keep me company. I had refused, but this particular night was stormy with pelting rain beating hard against the house.

I asked her to stay, and she readily agreed rather than face the onslaught outside. I poured some hot sake for us as a calming brace against what was happening outdoors. When I asked her about her life during the war years, she was at first reluctant to talk about it.

After a while she seemed anxious to unload her tale. She said, "As a schoolgirl, I was forced to learn English after the occupying forces took over the region where I lived. I know that several of my friends had relationships with the GIs, and I knew some of the girls had been raped. I was so angry about this; I did not want to go!"

She sobbed and sobbed as she spoke. She told me that her friends used to hide in the woods to keep from being found by any of the soldiers. She cried even more as she talked, and I felt shame and anger that she had gone through this experience. I felt she was going through a catharsis by sharing with me that she also had been raped.

From the depths of me I felt her pain and came to the conclusion she had indeed experienced a violation that had left deep scars. I was enraged that these things could happen, but I was becoming aware of all the atrocities of war, not just those on the battlefield.

Chapter 4

Life in Japan at Yokota Air Base seemed quite bright for a time. This country was beautiful with a calmness and serenity that I miss till this day. I miss the years of old traditions and ceremonies with family values and respect while having people bow to you to show that respect. While in Japan, we were happy to have seen the outstanding display of pink cherry blossoms in the spring, the fertility festival in the summer, and Kabuki Theater in the fall. We traveled to snow-topped Mt. Fuji and crowded, chaotic Tokyo and ate in lots of great restaurants. We took hot baths and had our backs scrubbed and walked on. We were entertained by beautiful black-haired geisha and shopped till we dropped. It was a cultural experience on a grand scale.

Of course, we lived the routine life as well. Ben was in the clinic and the flight surgeon's office practicing general medicine and loving every moment. He cared for people and enjoyed having the satisfaction of being there to help them solve their problems. He loved his patients and couldn't have been happier. We socialized with other young couples, and I kept busy taking courses in Chinese cooking and Japanese flower arranging. And who could forget those twenty-five-cent drinks at the O Club. Since we had a babysitter, we took advantage of those twenty-five centers and tried to catch all the shows that made the club circuit in the Far East. However, after a few drinks and an entertainer's rendition of "San Francisco," the tears flowed, and we always pined for home.

The flight surgeons did a lot of traveling, so it was not long before Ben received orders to pack his bags and kiss me good-bye. It was already fall of 1963, and all I could be told was that he would be gone for a couple of months. I was not permitted to know where he would be deployed. It was scary for me, but each time he left on an assignment, I grew up a little bit more. I was forced to rely only on myself for decision making, and during that time all the responsibility of the children was mine. I had no family for support—I was it. Friends were there for me, but I came to realize that I was really okay with it all. At least I thought I was, until that morning of November 22, 1963.

Our maid came through the door shouting, "Kennedy is dead! Kennedy is dead!"

"Oh, the president's father died?" I asked. No, that was not the case she told me. It was the president who was dead. He had been shot.

I thought she had it all wrong. I kept trying to correct her until my friend called, and I found out the awful truth. I was in shock. Everyone was in shock. Some friends came over, and we huddled by a radio to hear the details on an English-speaking station. It was at this time that I longed for Ben to be at home with me. The whole base was in an uproar, and it was then that I learned where Ben was. He was in New Delhi, the hot, hectic capitol of India and could not come home. So I dealt with all the chaos after Kennedy's death, wishing it had not happened. Months later, the Japanese people erected a beautiful memorial on the base. We all went to the dedication, which was attended by Robert Kennedy. Apparently JFK was quite respected in Japan, for it was a lovely tribute. I felt so sad. I felt sad for our dead president, for our country, for the war, for all the killing, and sad for myself.

Just when I was sure depression was going to claim me as a victim, as it had so many of the other wives, Ben returned home. Not only did he bring himself home but he also brought all kinds of goodies from India with him. When he unpacked, our living room looked like a crowded, oriental bazaar. Brassware, dolls, jewelry, silk saris, carved wooden screens, and oriental rugs filled the room. I was bursting with delight. Who said that acquiring material things was a bad thing? Everything was special, and these gifts continue to be some of my most beloved treasures.

I lovingly listened to the stories of his adventures in India. I learned through his films how very poor this country was and through photographs how incredibly beautiful it was. It was a huge challenge for a new doctor and he seemed to step up to the pressure. Of course, luck played a big part also. He was sent to India because Chinese troops were amassing on the northern border. His first assignment was to set up a MASH unit in New Delhi, to ensure that all the deployed troops had safe water to drink, and, most importantly, to make sure Coca Cola would be available. Jefferson Medical School had never trained him for any of this, but he figured it out. He arranged for fresh, clean water to be brought in by truck. When he had to inspect the local Coca Cola bottling company, he gave it a passing grade. Everything looked all right until he left by the back door and saw that all the water used to manufacture the coke was being piped in from the local river. The river was the same one where all the sewers emptied into. So, the Air Force had to have the military's favorite drink shipped all the way from the States. It was a job well done! There were other difficult parts of the mission that had to be overcome. Ben and the industrious guys in his unit gave it their all and played a big part in making the deployment very successful. For his extra effort, his unit won an award, and he was awarded the Air Force Commendation Medal—he was happy and proud, indeed.

The Vietnam War continued to rage, and Ben continued his practice of medicine at the clinic. Taking care of the jet jockeys was becoming more of a task because, as the war dragged on, they had more problems. Drugs were being misused to try to take the pain of war away. Some young soldiers were coming back without limbs, and depression was a rampant malady. It was life in the shadow of Vietnam, yet we both tried to enjoy the life we had. In one aspect it was tough because we were in the midst of a war and missed our families and friends, but in other ways we were on a privileged journey. We appreciated it for what it was and tried to see as much of our adopted country as we could.

The beauty of our surroundings was awesome. We took trips with the boys as often as we could, and when Ben was given some time off for rest and relaxation, we chose to get on one of the transport planes that went back and forth to the island of Guam. We were put in VIP quarters on the base and each day took the boys to the deserted stretch of pristine, white, sugar-like sand. It was so much fun. The aqua water was warm and calm, so we were able to navigate a small, yellow rubber raft in shallow water. We built sand castles that seemed to reach to the sky and dug holes that went almost to China. The weird thing, though, was the whole time we were at the beach, I had a feeling someone was watching us. The beach was surrounded on one side by jagged rocks and deep caves, and I had the creepy feeling that eyes were looking at us from the direction of the caves. I mentioned it to Ben, but he laughed it off.

We loved the week at the beach but imagine my amazement several days later, after we returned home, when I saw the headline in the Armed Forces paper *Stars and Stripes*, "JAPANESE SOLDIER CAPTURED IN CAVE ON ISLAND OF GUAM." After the war, a soldier had hidden in the caves around Guam and for twenty years had survived by stealing food and drink from garbage on the base. He did not know World War II had ended and was in a time warp. We followed the headlines with personal interest as this modern day Rip Van Winkle was indoctrinated into the 1960's. It was amazing. I just knew someone was watching us!

Ben continued to work hard in the flight surgeon's office. He thoroughly enjoyed seeing his Air Force dependent patients and being involved in all the action of the flight surgeon's office, when he was seeing officers and enlisted personnel. It was the kind of medicine he loved. He never wanted to specialize in any one branch of medicine, but felt his needs were fulfilled by doing general care. He had been urged many times to take a residency in a medical specialty because he could make more money, but it was just not what he wanted. I think at that period of time he wanted to stay in the service and continue to see designated patients and practice medicine using his diversified knowledge without any hassle. I had basically wanted what he wanted, except that I really would have liked to leave the Air Force eventually and settle in a nice, small town somewhere in the northeast part of the States. I still had that '50s mentality and dreamed of a house with a white picket fence and a comfortable life in a close-knit community where the doctor and his wife could be the center of the universe — truly a dream that never did quite happen.

Chapter 5

We still managed to do a lot of sightseeing and had taken a tour of Tokyo. While we were enchanted by a demonstration of a Japanese tea ceremony, we met Lin and Haley, a charming, young Chinese couple from Hong Kong. Haley was breathtakingly beautiful: slim with long, black, straight, silky hair and a soft voice. Lin was handsome and distinguished-looking with black, slicked-back hair and black-framed spectacles. They were on their honeymoon and told us he was training to be a pediatrician; she was a school teacher. How coincidental was that? Ben was a doctor and I was a school teacher.

We told them of our life on the base, and they were most surprised to learn that we actually had two cars. We listened to their life experiences and realized, although we had a lot in common, we led very different lives. Since they still had a few days left before they had to be home, we invited them to come back with us and spend those days at our house on the base. They were delighted, and we spent two fun-filled days showing them different sights around the Japanese countryside and the American base. After they returned to Hong Kong, we wrote letters and sent pictures for over a year. Then we decided to take a week's vacation in Hong Kong and made our reservation at a fairly nice hotel. We called our friends to tell them of our plans and were very excited about seeing one another again. We arrived at our hotel and I started to unpack. Ben dialed our friends' number, and when Lin answered, he told us he would be right over. We were unpacked when he arrived, but he told us to repack. He was taking us to their apartment; he wanted us to stay with them.

We totally protested, but Lin said, "If you are invited to a Chinese home and you refuse, that is an insult."

So, we repacked and went home with Lin to begin a fascinating week in Hong Kong.

After we arrived at our friends' apartment in a lovely, upscale part of the city and after all the hugging and kissing was over, we were shown to our room and bath. Then we were told that all the residences of Hong Kong were under a drought warning and that bathing was only allowed every third night for a short period of time. The water was turned off all other times, so no one could even cheat! Of course, drinking water would be saved and bathtubs would be filled to wash clothes. We could live with this and were still so happy to be with our friends in this incredible city. Lin and Haley had to work, so Ben and I were on our own during the day to explore everything in this different culture.

We were awed by the stark, crisp, modern architecture of some of the buildings in contrast to the shabby, impoverished sampans that sat lazily on the river. Each sampan looked like there were two or more families crowded onto and living on each boat, and the stench in that area was almost unbearable. The contrast of living was quite clear, and the density of people was beyond belief. We visited a leper colony and were completely blown away! People of all ages, including little toddlers, wandered around in varying stages of their disease. Those more advanced were without body parts. Eyes and noses were missing from some faces. The children had crusted areas over their bodies that were in various stages of leprosy. It was a sight that would haunt me for years. Our instinct was to reach out to them, but we thought better of it. It was very sad and heart wrenching. Years later we learned, happily, that new medical advances were being made to treat that disease and what we experienced would shortly be a thing of the past.

We explored every nook and cranny of the city and came back to the apartment each evening overheated, exhausted, and with feet in pain. Haley was raised in a very affluent family with servants, so she never learned to cook. Every night they would eat out at various local restaurants and, of course, we would go with them. Dinner was a three hour affair, and Lin insisted on doing all the ordering.

When I wanted to know exactly what we were eating, he said, "Before you get on the plane to go home, I will answer any questions you have about the food you ate." That was okay with me!

Since Lin had insisted on paying for all the meals, we felt quite guilty. I volunteered to cook a meal at their apartment one night and suggested they invite Haley's parents who lived nearby. It was set up, and I went off to a local Chinese market to purchase some things to put a meal together. To my dismay, I was not familiar with most of what was being sold. I did find some noodles, fresh tomatoes, garlic, lettuce, olive oil, vinegar, ground beef, and crusty Chinese rolls.

Back at the apartment, Haley's parents had already arrived. They did not speak English, so there was no conversation as I went to the kitchen to begin cooking. Haley was setting the table with her mother, and her father followed me into the kitchen and watched every move I made as I prepared, what turned out to be, a very good meal. He was smiling and nodding his head the whole time. He helped me carry the food out to the table, and after everyone sat down and said they were enjoying their dinner, I looked around and had to laugh. What was a nice Jewish girl doing in the middle of Hong Kong, cooking an Italian meal that we were eating with chopsticks in a Chinese home?

When it was time to leave, Lin and Haley took us to the airport. I was anxious to ask Lin about all the food we had so bravely eaten. I described a few meals, and he told me what the food had been. We had devoured one-hundred-year-old eggs, grasshoppers, all kinds of exotic fish, and finally he told me about the night we had eaten dog! I thought he was kidding, but indeed he was not. When I began to make gyrations like I was going to vomit he asked, "Well, how did it taste?"

I stopped to recall and answered, "Like chicken."

"Case closed." he retorted.

Chapter 6

The week we were back on the base the craziest thing happened. At two o'clock in the morning, while we were in bed and sleeping, I was woken up by what seemed to be voices coming from under our bed. The bedroom was black, in total darkness. I lay very still and listened to the voices, which were clearly two men shouting at each other in Japanese. I totally freaked out! How could there possibly be Japanese men under our bed? But I clearly heard their chatter; my stomach was turning over. I elbowed Ben until he woke up and told him to listen for the voices.

He thought I was out of my mind, but then said, "I hear them. I hear them!"

We were both paralyzed with fear. Finally, I started to poke his back and forced him to look under the bed. To our relief no one was there, but we easily figured out that the voices were actually coming from a crawl space underneath the house. So, my very brave husband got up and grabbed the baseball bat from the boys' room and proceeded to tiptoe, in his underwear, to the back door.

He opened the back door and started to yell, "Come out of there! What are you doing under my house? I'm going to knock you silly with this bat. My wife is calling the MPs."

Well, two little, adorable Japanese men crawled out of the crawl space, bowing and begging in English for Ben not to hit them. They told us they had been sent to fix the heat in the residential area of the base and the end of the line was under our house. The whole scene at this point was so funny that as they ran from our house, we totally cracked up. They did, thank goodness, manage to fix the heat.

The Vietnam War raged on and Ben continued to fly in and out of that country. In between that and sitting on the flight pad in Korea, he saw patients on the base, his favorite part of the whole job. As a flight surgeon he was also on a team sent out to investigate a plane crash, and it wasn't long before he was called to leave on a mission of investigation. A transport plane had crashed into the mountains in a very remote area of north Japan, and his team was being sent there. The site was a lush green dense part of northern Japan where the ground seemed to drink up the rain. Everything was built on mud. The people of the nearby Japanese village had never seen an American, so an interpreter had to be sent with the crash team. The only way to get to this village was by helicopter, which was dangerous at best.

They arrived during the rainy season and walking was hazardous. Slipping and sliding was unavoidable even when wearing Air Force combat boots. (Japanese people wear platform sandals to keep their socks and feet dry). The team was housed in the local residents' fairly primitive, thatched-roof houses and had to set out each day by foot to climb straight up the mountain and reach the crash site.

They worked ten hours every day for weeks in grueling conditions of rain, mud, and mudslides. At night, they enjoyed a unique experience of being able to eat with their host families who did not speak a word of English, but who gave their all to cook the best of Japanese home cooking. The routine was up at 5 a.m. and to bed by 8 p.m. But the best part was at the end of every day when each of the five men on the team received a hot bath and massage from various people in the village. The men were treated with great respect and were always bowed to in a traditional manner. They gave that respect back by bowing and smiling often at the men and women who catered to their every need. They completed their mission and were able to retrieve and bag the pilots' bodies, recover personal items to bring back to family members, and determine what caused the horrific crash into the mountain. They had managed to invade this remote village with honor and humility, leaving a memory of favorable impressions.

We were surprised and stunned! As we walked into the home of our friends, after Ben's return, thinking we were going to a dinner party to celebrate a birthday, it hit us. The party was really a surprise farewell party given for us by our friends before we left Japan. The room was swathed in white toilet paper with the words "Good-bye B. M. and Bobbie" printed all over. We cracked up! B. M. stood for Benjamin Matthew but had a very funny connotation as a party decoration. Our friends had been pretty clever and creative!

The evening was so bittersweet and nostalgic. Hysterical laughing and crying were all part of our good-byes. It would be two weeks before our departure for the States and we had sad feelings about leaving.

In his short speech Ben said it quite well, "I have mixed emotions about leaving my adopted country. Living in Japan for three years has been an extraordinary experience. I will miss this beautiful country, my Air Force buddies, and my Japanese friends as well. I've grown so much as a person and matured as a physician. I have become better. I have become more worldly. I have become smarter. In three years of medical experience, I have become a more tolerant and caring physician. I have learned to live my life wrapped around the lives of others who are in need. I hope I served them well and used my accumulated knowledge to make a difference. I pray this is not naïve. Thanks for being my friends and putting up with all those late or canceled dates and grouchy episodes when my patients were not doing well. I love you all and have just one request...that we don't lose touch, ever!"

Two weeks later we were gone, taking with us the best memories of a lifetime.

The twenty-six hours on the plane returning to the States were just as brutal as our journey to Japan. This time we had two toddlers with us, and the trip seemed like a three-ring circus. We had decided before the trip that we needed help getting the kids to sleep and our new friend this time was going to be Benadryl, which was intended to put the children in dreamland for at least a few hours of our choosing. Benadryl is an antihistamine given to children for colds and allergies, but parents had discovered its sedative side effect, and I'm embarrassed to say that we were going to try to take advantage of it. The problem was we did not pay attention to all the instructions (something that Ben stressed to his patients to do). The dosage was to be determined by the weight of the patient. After twelve hours, we had eaten three different meals, plus ten snacks, read lots of books, played games, and crayoned a picture for every passenger aboard. We sang and cuddled, and then it was time for Benadryl. Ten minutes after plump, little Scott (who was three) took his dosage, he happily fell asleep. Ten hours after thin, little Michael (who was two) took his dosage, he was still hyperactive and running up and down the aisle or squirming and crying on my lap. It was a plane ride from hell!

Our family happily arrived in San Francisco, however, and landed at Travis Air Force Base where we disembarked. We walked about 500 feet from the plane, and then I did something that must have seemed quite dramatic but was an important symbol to me. I bent down on my knees and kissed the ground I stood on.

I was happy and overwhelmed to be back on US soil, and I muttered, "Thank you, God, for bringing us safely home."

While we waited to clear customs, several of the airport customs' guards were asking questions about what we missed most, other than family and friends, after being out of the country for such a long time. I knew that answer in a second so I responded quickly. First, I missed good hamburgers and hot dogs, and second, I sorely missed supermarkets. Third, I missed William B. Williams.

"Who in the world is William B. Williams?" they questioned.

"Oh, that must be an East Coast thing." I explained. "He's a silk-voiced DJ, broadcasting the *Make Believe Ballroom* out of a New York radio station. He plays all the popular music, and I really missed listening to him and all the moods he creates."

Funny, the things you hold dear.

We were quartered in an officer's apartment and started the Air Force departure process. Then we received an unscheduled phone call from our friend, Tim, who worked in the Air Force Surgeon General's office. He was a Colonel in charge of physician recruitment for the Air Force and was very good at his job. He told Ben that the higher-ups wanted him to stay and sign as a career officer. Apparently Ben had caught the attention of some of the officers at the command level when he won his medals and had worked so seriously hard in the medical clinic. Tim said that they would make it very attractive if he would stay.

After half a dozen of these calls with Tim promising the moon, we started to pay attention. He offered Ben his choice of any base in the United States as an assignment and seemed pretty sure that if Ben agreed and was career minded, he could set his sights on attaining the rank of general in the Medical Corps. This was mind boggling! We had enjoyed our time in the Air Force but weren't sure if it would appeal to us for the next twenty years. Ben was very conflicted. I was willing to do whatever would make him happy but really did not cherish the idea of constantly moving around for the next twenty years. It was hard thinking of his charging off to all the hot spots in the world if he were needed. I still pictured that white picket-fenced house in a nice little town in New Jersey.

This was a new wrinkle in our lives and we didn't know what to do. Then Tim made us another offer. He would send Ben to Dover Air Force Base in Delaware, fairly close to our families. Ben would have to sign up for one more year and would be made Chief of Aviation Medicine. During that time, we could wrap our heads around this new idea and make up our minds. We agreed.

Chapter 7

Dover Air Force Base was a small base in the state of Delaware. It was very important during the Vietnam War because most of the dead bodies were shipped back to the Dover base, which functioned as a military morgue. To this day, it continues to assume this role and guarantees, to the fallen warriors, a return home full of dignity and grace.

Ben was put right to work in the flight surgeon's office. It wasn't long until he was once more being deployed to areas in different parts of the world. We had a tough time accepting this and explaining it to our families, who couldn't understand why Ben would stay in the Air Force at all and not want to start his civilian career. There were times we did not know either, but we knew that we had to take a chance at finding out if this life was going to be for us.

We were happy to move into a lovely, traditional, two-story brick house with a big yard and a large, child-friendly playground across the street. Our kids loved their new surroundings. The houses in the officer's area were basically the same: a good size and fine looking. The base exchange was well-stocked, and there was plenty of good shopping off the base. The town of Dover is quaint and old fashioned. It seemed a safe place to take a stroll at night. There was a reason "lower" Delaware was called "slower" Delaware, and it wasn't a bad thing. Our neighbors and new friends all came from various bases around the globe, so conversation was always lively and stimulating when we got together. The war was usually the first topic of discussion. Sometimes, arguments ensued and tempers were hot. I remember a particular party at the Matlin's, our neighbors across the street.

"Why the hell should we still be there at all?" Colonel Matlin said, with the veins in his neck popping out." We were only supposed to go there as advisors, and now we are in a full-fledged war."

Soft-spoken Captain Peters rose to the defense of the government.

"So you would just let the Communists run over that country? The next thing you know they would be over in this country, and we would have to fight them on our soil."

This dialogue continued for hours with everyone wanting to say his or her piece. Of course, adding fuel to the fire was the fact that Colonel Matlin was a martini aficionado, and ice-cold gin was poured into everyone's iced martini glass as soon as two sips were taken. It was almost a ritual; iced pitchers were kept in the refrigerator between servings. The Colonel was kind of a bigwig on the base, and no one wanted to offend him. A lot of martinis were consumed!

Many volatile discussions were going on. Just like in the rest of the country, the pros and cons of the war discussed were passionate. I was not much of a gin drinker but did not want to be impolite. As a matter of fact, since Ben and I were the youngest ones at this party of captains, majors, colonels, and generals, plus wives, I really wanted to impress our neighbors and their guests. The problem was that as I sat there, sipping, I realized the room was starting to spin around me. I quickly assessed the situation and figured out that if I held onto various pieces of furniture as I made my way across the room, I could make it all the way to the door and manage a polite and gracious exit. My plan worked fine. I said my smiling good-byes, opened the door with ease and poise, casually stepped out onto the small entrance patio, took a step, and proceeded to slip on the snow that had just fallen and land face down in a heap of new snow as everyone watched from the big picture window. I was mortified, but learned two lessons: one, stop trying to impress people; and two, don't drink martinis.

Being in the military in a sense sheltered us from civilian problems. There was always a check forthcoming, and we were surrounded by people who were like family. It was life in a cocoon, which we were really getting used to. But there was always the question of whether we needed to experience civilian life and have Ben experience the practice of medicine in the real world. Medicine had started to change since Ben had arrived in Dover and not for the better. The docs frequently joked that they were soon going to be working for the biggest HMO (Health Maintenance Organization) in the free world. They had all the advantages, but the pay was about half of civilian doctors, and they were assuming more and more responsibilities. Patients were coming to the ER at any time with non-emergent ailments and to the clinics with every little ache and pain. Wait times were hours instead of minutes now, and it took months to see a specialist. It was becoming socialized medicine at its worst.

Ben decided to study and take the examination for a New Jersey medical license. New Jersey was our home state where he would have most liked to practice. We were back to hardly spending any time together, as he hit the books every night after a full day's work at the clinic. After about six months of study, we made the trip to New Jersey and deposited the kids with my parents, Grandma Lily and Grandpa Al. We checked into a seedy, old motel in Trenton, the capitol, where the exam was to be held. For three days, while all the candidates' medical knowledge was being tested, I just hung around the motel and watched TV or read. When it was over, we headed home, where three months of anxious, nervous waiting began. When the letter came notifying Ben that he had passed the exam and was now being awarded a New Jersey state medical license, we were happy and scared!

I don't think scared aptly describes exactly how we were really feeling. We were petrified and in a total panic state. We had made the choice to leave the Air Force and were faced with some cold facts. We would shortly have no income, no plan as to how to have an income, no house, and two toddlers and ourselves to clothe and feed. However, we had dreams for our future, and clinging to that thought, we put all our belongings in storage and traveled to New Jersey to begin the rest of our life's journey.

"What town are we going to settle in? Where is your practice going to be? Will we have enough money to buy a house? Do we have to buy office equipment?" I was hammering Ben with questions as we nervously drove toward New Brunswick, New Jersey, which was in the area where Ben had grown up.

"Relax, I have everything under control, and I have a few surprises for you," Ben calmly said.

Apparently I was the nervous one.

"I have an interview with Johnson and Johnson, the huge pharmaceutical company, in the morning. They have their corporate headquarters in New Brunswick. They're looking for a part-time medical director for one of their facilities, the Eastern Surgical Dressing Plant. A friend told me about the open position, and I sent them my resume. If I could snag that position for the mornings, then we could survive while I built up my practice in the afternoons. I like the idea of practicing solo so I can do medicine my way. Now, get this, my parents found an area where they are building new houses. The development sits on a hill, and the first house is a corner house with an entrance in the front of the house and on the side. It may have a lot of potential for a house/office combo."

The dream was starting to take shape, and I thought I might get my white picket fence after all.

Frankly, we did not know what we were doing, but we had started to overcome our fears and rode forward like settlers conquering the West. Everything then started to happen. The recruiters at Johnson and Johnson liked Ben's Air Force experience in preventive and occupational medicine and hired him to be the medical director of their Eastern Surgical Dressings Plant. We went to see the site of the new house construction and fell in love with it. Mostly young families with small children were buying these homes. Then the wheels started turning.

"This would be a really good base of patients for a medical practice," Ben observed.

So we chose the model home with front and side entrances to build on a corner lot and made a down payment to secure our first real home and Ben's first real office. The house was not that big but the builder worked magic with the extra space on the side. The new houses were devoid of style for the most part, so we tried to add some accent to ours. We had wrought iron posts, black shutters, and a red door put on the front of a grey shingled house. On the side, we put a black canopy over the office door to distinguish it from our living space. In only eight weeks we had a lovely home and an inviting office. We landscaped with lots of trees, bushes, and flowers, making it look lovely. I never did get my white picket fence, but an elegant black wrought iron fence made the property spectacular. The builder, Mr. Scarpone, even presented us with a sign and post which he set into the walk in front of the office, announcing Ben's name and specialty: Benjamin M. Kaminski, M.D., Family and Occupational Medicine.

"I have just one more thing," he said." I want to be your first patient."

Ben was thrilled and happily granted his request.

Chapter 8

It was 1965, with still no ceasefire in Vietnam, the war that refused to end. It was also the year of the real beginning of my husband's career in private medicine. The town we decided to build his practice in was Piscataway, New Jersey.

When we sent out postcards announcing our location for the opening and our change of residence, one of our cousins called and jokingly said, "Piss-cataway...What kind of name is that? I don't think I want to come to visit."

I retorted not thinking she was at all funny, "I'll have you know this town was named after a brave and honored Indian tribe by the name of the Piscatawa Indians. Their chief was a respected medicine man. So it may be completely appropriate that we are here. He and his ancestors were probably buried near or even under our house."

Well, it was just her little joke, and the truth was they visited often, especially when someone had a medical problem.

The next few months were chaotic. We moved our furniture and belongings into the house part of our property and furnished the office with comfortable new office furniture and modern medical equipment. I had a ball decorating everything. We placed ads in the local papers to find and employ a nurse and receptionist. Ben had a suite comprised of a waiting room, office, two exam rooms, powder room, and reception room. It was not huge but perfect enough to accommodate a small medical practice. We sent out notices announcing the opening of the practice to people in the neighborhood, local doctor's offices, hospitals, the Chamber of Commerce, and all sorts of organizations.

Ben was anxious to shout, "Look, world, I am here! Here I am!"

Ben applied to two local hospitals for privileges and received acceptance at both. The surprise was when we found out about the selection process. A never-disclosed or admitted-to point system was in place, and Ben received points for the quality of the medical school he attended and, amongst other things, if he or his family came from the local area. I wonder if that system is still in place today.

From the get-go, we were aware of all the politics of the medical community. The office was not yet open when Ben received a call one evening while we were having dinner. It was the operator from the answering service he had recently signed onto, telling him about a patient waiting to see him at the hospital.

"But I don't have any patients," he said. "How could the patient be asking for me?"

"Well, you're the doctor that Dr. Reid signed out to for the weekend," she told him.

"What? No doctor ever called to ask me if I would take his coverage this weekend, but I won't abandon this patient. I'll be right over." He looked at me, shrugged, and left.

On Monday morning he called Dr. Reid. Ben was clearly put out with him. Reid told Ben that the older doctors simply just signed out to the newer, younger docs and that was how it was in the community.

"Well, it's not how it is with me," Ben told him. "In the future, I would appreciate a call asking me if I am available and giving me a choice." Needless to say that doctor never became a friendly colleague, but they did work out an agreement for coverage when needed by each of them.

Ben was young, principled, high-spirited, and full of ideas about how medicine should be practiced. He had just come away from a situation where he was top dog and in charge. Sometimes his idealism didn't jive with the way things were always done. At the time, I prayed that he hadn't shot himself in the foot.

Ben started working at Johnson and Johnson and was already working at the free clinic in the hospital the month the office opened. What a wonderful program the free clinic was. If it were still in place today, no one would be without health care. It worked like this: in order to be on staff at the hospital, the doctors each had to volunteer at the clinic for twelve hours per month. The doctors were happy to donate their time to the community. If patients could verify that they were in a situation and had no insurance and could not afford to pay, they were accepted to the clinic. Patients could see any doctor on staff, and it also meant that if they happened to need surgery, they could have any one of the fine surgeons on staff operate. Because the hospital was a community hospital, fundraising helped to defray expenses, and the government paid for any shortfall. No person in need was turned away, and there was no such thing as anyone without proper health care. It amazed me that when big HMOs and insurance companies began to rule the country, these wonderful programs went down the tubes. What a shame!

We had last minute things to do at the office, so we zeroed in on the hours of one to five for Ben to see patients when he spent his mornings at Johnson and Johnson. Although all the doctors in town closed one day a week, usually Wednesday presumably to play golf, he made the decision to stay open the whole week and only be available on weekends for emergencies. He wanted to spend time with his boys. I think he remembered old Dr. Smith's words of wisdom. Before we could get a marriage license in 1960, we were both required to have blood tests and a physical exam.

Afterward the doctor had advice for both of us. "Bobbie, I want to tell you never to become Mrs. Doctor," he cautioned, "Ben, you must remember this. The day after you die every one of your patients will get good, competent care."

We got it! Those words stayed with us Ben's entire career.

We hired a big, jolly, red-haired angel by the name of Mary Bolati, RN. She wanted to take the job of nurse and receptionist and announced she would be calling Ben "Dr. K." instead of Dr. Kaminski. There was no doubt she could handle it. She was a nice, gentle, take-charge person but could not start work the same week we booked the first patient, so I helped out until she came on board. Of course, the very first patient was our builder Mr. Scarpone. He was so glad to be in the office that it was a bit difficult to understand what his complaints were, as he was speaking in half English and half Italian. Ben managed to elicit the info and sent him home elated to be number one. Five other new patients came that day including a neighbor from across the street. Mrs. Braunstein called to say that she had been exposed to hepatitis and was told she needed a shot.

"I'm so glad you are here in the neighborhood," she said. This will make things so easy for me." Ben told her she needed a blood test and an injection.

"Where do you give me the shot?" she asked with concern in her voice.

"In your tush," he said.

"Oh no, I can't let you give me the shot there and let you see my tush. I've known you and your family since you were a little boy.

I'm embarrassed to let you see my tush."

"Listen, Mrs. Braunstein, in my short career I have seen hundreds of tushes, and frankly they are all the same to me. No offense, but if you've seen one tush, you've seen them all. So let's get on with it."

She laughed, had her shot, went home, and became a very loyal patient.

Medical school in those days did not prepare its students for the real world. There were no business courses given to clue in the doctors as to how to begin or run a medical practice. It was, as they say, root hog root. If one was lucky enough to have a friend or relative to turn to for advice, then it was easier. If not, there was a lot of trial by error. At the startup of the office we did not even know what to charge for office visits or procedures. So Ben called his colleagues to see what they were charging. They told him they could not tell him as it was against the law. It was considered price-fixing. We thought they were all out of their minds. So, I just called every office in town, posing as a patient and asked what the charge for an office visit was. Then we made up a fee schedule within the range of quoted fees and posted it in the waiting room.

We hung another framed article that cleverly described Ben's philosophy of medicine. It was the story of a stranger who came to a nice little town and considered staying. He walked around town and came to a cliff at the edge of town. The drop over the cliff was steep and dangerous. He went to the mayor and told him that the town should put up a fence or barrier because someone could fall over and be seriously hurt or die. There was no need to spend money for a fence, the stranger was told, because waiting at the bottom of the cliff was the town's finest ambulance.

The story very aptly delivered Ben's message about preventive medicine. The medical world seemed locked into spending the healthcare dollar on the sick and dying patient instead of programs to prevent the patient from getting sick in the first place. Indeed, why put up a preventive fence if an ambulance could whisk you away to be treated at a hospital. Hospitals were happy if beds could be filled. The drug companies were happy. The insurance companies could pick and choose what treatment they would pay for and how much they would pay. The so-called insurance statistics could not validate preventive testing. They were not cost-effective. After all, as an example, if a routine test yielded only one person out of one hundred showing cancer that should not substantiate the testing. Too bad if that person is a loved one.

Like Hansel and Gretel following a path of crumbs home, patients found a path to the new office. Ben was delighted, yet overwhelmed. Mary had started her duties as office nurse, and the combination of an eager young doctor and his personable, proficient nurse seemed to be just what the patients wanted. They needed a nurse who was friendly and helpful, and they wanted a doctor who would listen to them. Office visits were scheduled for no less than fifteen minutes, and Dr. K.'s policy was that new patients had to have a screening physical exam which took about an hour. This was part of his successful preventive medicine program.

Patients received counseling about habits that could lead to chronic illness. They were given pamphlets on causes of disease and encouraged to make lifestyle changes. All this was pretty radical in the '60s and '70s, and it took a lot of persuading on the doctor's part. But it worked. Patients trusted the doctor and seemed eager to comply. Dr. K.'s hospital census was almost nonexistent.

Soon office hours had to be extended as the patient visits increased in the first year. Best of all, the doctor and his nurse were enjoying the immensely laid-back, home-style practice, which very closely resembled episodes of Marcus Welby, a popular TV show that aired from 1969 to 1976. It was the most popular doctor show on television because it deviated from the others by showing an office setting instead of a hospital setting. Viewers followed cases of patients who had everyday chronic illness versus onetime emergency problems. The cases delved more into the psychological aspects and personal problems causing various illnesses. Much like the real medical practice of Dr. K., the emphasis was on causation of disease and its prevention. So timing was just right for Dr. Welby and Dr. K.

I now worked in the office part-time as the receptionist. I was working the day an unusual incident happened. As always, if the doctor had a female patient in the exam room, the nurse would chaperone. On this particular day a young woman had come in just to talk to the doctor, and so I ushered her into Dr. K.'s office, where she could comfortably sit across from the doctor at his desk, instead of the exam room. The nurse was busy with another patient. Mindful of the protocol suggested by the malpractice insurance companies,

I kept the office door ajar so I could see the patient from my desk. This was before HIPAA (the Health Insurance Portability and Accountability Act), the privacy rule implemented in 1996, which protects patient written medical information, verbal information, and visible information.

The patient was sobbing hysterically as she talked to the doctor, and in an empathetic gesture, he reached across the desk and patted her hand, "Everything will turn out all right," he said, as he finished patting her hand several times.

Whatever advice he gave her seemed to stop her tears, and she thanked him and came out to get her follow-up appointment from me.

That evening we received a telephone call at home from a caller who identified himself as the husband of the young woman, crying in the office that day. I could hear him shouting through the speaker phone and accusing Ben of making advances toward his wife.

"You were holding my wife's hand," he screamed. We looked at each other puzzled and stunned.

"I assure you I was just trying to calm her and offer her support." The man continued his assault until Ben told him, "Listen, my wife witnessed the entire encounter."

Then, he stopped yelling.

He didn't apologize, but just said he didn't want his wife ever seeing any professionals and slammed down the phone. The episode was scary but reinforced the fact that the malpractice insurance companies are correct. There are a lot of crazy people looking for trouble. Of course, it didn't stop Ben from giving his patients, especially the elderly ones, a hug now and again.

The next few years were fairly routine. Ben continued his position at Johnson and Johnson, which gave him some diversity in occupational medicine and a more or less prestigious standing in the community. His practice was very busy and he seemed quite content. A cross section of patients came to the office from the very young (five years and up) to the very old (ninety-five years and down). It was a true suburban, general practice. In the service, patients were restricted to Air Force personnel and dependents. In the real world, there was a potpourri of patients from all walks of life and all socioeconomic backgrounds. It was this, I believe, that made medicine so eclectic and challenging for Ben. As a general physician, he needed to know something about everything in the medical world.

We took a lot of vacation time off, but this was mostly paired with a lecture or seminar about current medical topics. Ben tried to keep up-to-date and ahead of the curve. However, rest and relaxation were also key, and when the patients would ask why the doctor would be taking so much vacation time and complain that they did not want to see any other physician when he was gone, my answer was standard.

"Wouldn't you want your doctor rested and relaxed when he saw you instead of harried and frazzled?" I would ask them.

They quickly caught on. But even when Ben was away from the practice, his seriously ill patients were still on his mind. He really showed concern above and beyond the call of duty, and I never knew him to totally relax.

The one thing his patients admired was his never-give-up attitude. If he came across symptoms in a patient not easily diagnosed or not textbook, he would pursue every avenue until an answer was found or a diagnosis made. It was known that Dr. K. would consult with specialists all over the country, if necessary, to get a handle on a puzzling medical problem. Knowing this, his patients felt secure and well-cared-for. This was the stone and mortar that built his fine reputation.

Sometimes a patient's diagnosis went beyond book knowledge and encompassed the doctor's medical intuition. There was the case of the twenty-seven-year-old woman who came to the office with complaints of severe abdominal pain. After blood tests and X-rays came back normal—keep in mind this was before CAT scans (computerized axial tomography) or MRIs (magnetic resonance imaging)—and a thorough exam was done, a diagnosis could not be made. So a consult for the following day was arranged with a trusted general surgeon.

The surgeon called, "I could not find anything. Her tests were all fine. I think her pain might be psychosomatic."

"I don't know," Ben told him. "My intuition tells me not to rule out stomach cancer."

But the surgeon disagreed and sent the patient back to Ben, saying he thought the patient was much too young for stomach cancer. Ben reexamined the patient and called the surgeon back.

"Something is not right and my gut feeling is that perhaps you need to do exploratory surgery. You need to probe further."

Lucky for the patient the surgeon did. Cancer of the stomach was found and removed in time for the young woman to be fully cured. The patient returned to see Ben in a few months with just a scar, a dozen roses for the staff, and a two-pound box of Godiva chocolates for the doctor — thankful for her life.

Chapter 9

One day nurse Mary, who had also become friend Mary, called upstairs to talk to me. "Bobbie, look out the window on the side of the house near the office and tell me what you see."

I looked and reported back, "I see a long, pink Cadillac. It's quite snazzy. Is it a patient's?"

"You bet it is," she replied. "It belongs to a slim, young, good-looking blonde who just happens to be a patient and is in the office for a visit right now and has eyes for your husband. She's flirting with him as we speak."

"Well, good luck to her. But if she wants him, he comes with kids." We both laughed and the incident passed.

I had made up a strict, enforced rule. I had to, in order to save myself. "I don't make lunch," I announced on the first day Ben started to practice.

I wanted a life and proclaimed my strong decree. Ben obliged and had a favorite sandwich shop that he would stop at on his way to the office after he left Johnson and Johnson around noontime. If the weather was nice, he would sometimes sit in the park adjacent to the shop and enjoy lunch. One afternoon he came into the house seemingly eager to talk.

"Bobbie, did you ever see a big pink Cadillac parked near our house during office hours?" I responded with an innocent and casual little white lie.

"No," I said.

"Well," he continued, "I was eating my sandwich in the park when my patient drove up in her Caddie. She made a big point of acting surprised to see me and told me that her apartment was located just across the street from the park. She then invited me to see her apartment and to finish my lunch there. When I politely refused, she kept insisting, but I begged off to come straight home. She then extended another invite for any time I wanted, and I went on my way."

"Oh, I'm sure she did, but don't get a swelled head," I said.

"Just keep in mind that you are a professional and an easy mark, so don't let her intimidate you. It's your choice if you continue to see her as a patient. Just be careful."

In my head, I believe I was also planning her murder. However, I didn't have to resort to violence because my friend and confidante in the office disclosed that the patient called to say she was moving out of town and to kiss the doctor good-bye for her. Sometimes life is far from being routine.

We had made friends with many of the couples in our immediate neighborhood, and many had also become patients. It was hard but necessary to keep friendships and patient care separate. Ben was very discreet and never mixed the two. That was his thinking even back when we were in Japan.

I recall a dinner dance at the O Club. Standing near the bar was an attractive, dark-haired woman. In her hand was a tropical-looking cocktail, and as we approached, she was trying very hard to hide the glass.

"I'm so sorry, Doctor, I know you told me no alcohol while I was on my medication," she admitted.

Very kindly he announced, "Listen, I don't mix my professional life and my social life. You're free to either take my advice or ignore it, but I will never mention anything that has to do with you as my patient in a social setting."

She seemed relieved and eager to introduce herself to me. I picked up on a definite southern drawl which was further defined when she introduced herself.

"Ma name is Trixie and I was bawn on the fawth of Julah in Selma, Alabama."

Trixie appreciated the fact that her doctor had not embarrassed her, and she and her husband became our friends for many years.

The fact that Ben was discreet (rightly so), and I was aware of this, did lead to some edgy moments. On one particular Sunday morning, I came down the stairs to begin my general cleanup of the house before I made breakfast. While I was straightening the family room, I noticed there was a large, glass ashtray on the coffee table with about a dozen, red lipstick-stained cigarette butts. I did not smoke and was very curious about where the cigarettes had come from. I also felt a bit anxious. Who had been in my house as I slept, and had Ben just accidently left the ashtray on the table? When Ben appeared, I confronted him.

He started to hem and haw. "Oh, they belong to a female patient of mine. She needed my help," he cautiously explained.

"When was she here?" I queried with a bit of apprehension. "I went to bed at twelve. I guess she was here later than that."

"Actually," he continued, "when I went to turn off the lights outside, I noticed a car parked near the office. I went out to investigate and discovered it was one of my patients sitting in her car, hysterically crying. I asked her what was up and was she all right. She said, 'I am sitting here thinking of killing myself.' She had been drinking. I coaxed her into leaving the car and coming inside the house to talk. I made her coffee and she smoked. We talked for an hour or so. It seems her husband was cheating on her and he wanted a divorce. She just wanted to kill herself. She had some of her medications with her and was going to swallow all of them. After reasoning with her, I called her girlfriend who came and got her, along with my prescribed referral to a psychiatrist. I hope it works."

Actually, it did work. She got her divorce and lived in our town with her children for many years. At that point, figuring in my encounter in Japan, Ben and I had a 1-1 tied score in warding off suicide attempts.

Our neighborhood was comprised of upscale families living in neat homes with meticulously manicured lawns. It was a great place to raise kids. The area consisted of fifty-six houses with one dead-end street and several branches of cul-de-sacs leading to the main street. It was safe and protected. We let our children play outside with no fear of them being harmed. It was a different time. There was a beautiful park with a friendly zoo across from our area, and the whole scene was a perfect picture of wholesome, suburban America. Or so it seemed. Apparently Ben and I were quite naïve in those days. How could we have known that in the quiet stillness of a seemingly made-in-heaven community there was a lot of hanky-panky going on? When I first heard the gossip, it was in sheer disbelief.

"What? There is a key club here in our development? Uh, what exactly is a key club?" I stupidly asked my friend Marsha. Marsha was my friend and walking partner, and I saw her every morning for our exercise routine. We talked as much as we walked, solving all the problems of the world.

She explained about the key club. "Couples have a party and at the beginning of the evening throw their house keys in a basket. Each couple picks out a set of keys and switches spouses for the night with the owners of the keys that were chosen. There you have it."

"Wow, what's wrong with those people? They have kids. What if the kids find out? They're setting some crazy moral standards."

Apparently it didn't all work out, because it wasn't long before two of the couples got divorces and the ex-husband of one couple married the ex-wife of another. It was messed up.

But life went on in our now near perfect neighborhood. Of course, it was the beginning of the '70s where "Do your own thing" was prevalent. Looking back, I'm not so sure that was a good plan.

"Do your own thing" was definitely the theme for a neighborhood party we were invited to. We usually received an invite to most of the parties in the complex, but this was to a home we had never been to before.

A hot, scrumptious-smelling barbeque and some cool jazz were in full swing when we arrived, and the tempting aroma of smoking pork and sweet barbeque sauce was in the air. But pork wasn't the only thing that was smoking. The group of people numbered about a dozen, and I noticed as we circulated around the patio that everyone was smoking cigarettes — not their own — but several that were being passed around. That was my first clue. Then when the tasty barbeque dinner was served, everyone relished each bite and was licking their fingers while making sounds of profound pleasure. It seemed strange to me. The barbeque was good but not that good. That was my second clue. When chocolate cake was served for dessert, the crowd went wild. The cake was devoured with inflated enthusiasm, and after that third clue, I concluded the real treat had been marijuana. Ben agreed. No one had passed a cigarette to us, so I guessed there was a conspiracy to exclude us. When I called to thank the hostess the next day, I received an apology in return.

"I know you were aware that we were all smoking pot last night," she confessed, "but we purposely didn't include you because we didn't want to put the doctor in a compromising situation. As a physician in the community with a good reputation, we know not to involve him, so we just bypassed you both. So, sorry, hope you were not uncomfortable."

"No, we were just fine," I assured her. At the time I was thinking that our perfect neighborhood was slowly going to hell or maybe "to pot."

Chapter 10

A new dimension of patient care began to take place in Ben's medical practice. He was seeing all the members of an entire family. It made his work a bit easier because he was able to observe the dynamics of a whole family and how they related to each other. He applied for and received what was necessary to become a Fellow in Family Medicine, awarded to doctors who make significant contributions in their field of medicine. His studying and learning was beyond ending, but he loved it. The more challenges, the more pleased he was. Besides becoming proficient in problems of the very young, he also took courses in geriatric medicine and thoroughly enjoyed his senior citizens. Due to his Air Force background, he qualified as a Federal Aviation Administration Examiner and was certified to do physical examinations on commercial, private, and student pilots. They needed these exams in order to get and renew their licenses, so he was feeling good taking care of flying personnel again. However, preventive medicine was still his thrust. Successfully so, I might add, as his schedule was always full. Patients sought him out as a physician who listened, took the extra diagnostic test, walked the extra mile for them, and was a darn good diagnostician.

Medicine in the early '70s was in a true state of flux. Medical technology changed, sometimes from week to week. Keeping up with the latest treatments, testing, and new medications became a huge undertaking for all practicing physicians. Our every weekend started to be taken up with courses and seminars in an effort to keep Dr. K. current. Then he would spend hours at night in our library studying all the latest information. At times Marvin, who was a patent attorney and husband of my friend Marsha, would come over and read at our house and borrow books from Ben's medical library. Often Ben and Marvin would have long discussions about medicine.

This went on for almost a year, after which one night Marvin declared, "I really always wanted to be a doctor, and I find your books and our talks so stimulating. Even though I will be forty years old soon, I've decided to go to medical school and am delighted about my decision."

We were glad for him. How brave and dedicated was that? Marvin was soon accepted to a medical school out West, and Marsha and Marvin gave up their home and good life as they knew it, so he could follow his dream and begin his new career. I was sad when they moved. I lost a walking partner but never lost my friend. When Marvin became a doctor, we were all thrilled.

Ben was hoping that Marvin might move back to New Jersey and perhaps join him in practice, but that wasn't in the cards. Solo practice was becoming overwhelming, and most new doctors were forming groups to share patient load and get good coverage. Our family time was dwindling. People expected doctors to fix every aspect of their lives and insisted on a pill to help whatever ailed them. At that time, most payment was fee for service. The patients paid for their visits, and the office staff would help them fill out papers so they could be reimbursed by their own insurance company if they had one. We were becoming overwhelmed with paperwork. Those patients on entitlement programs came to the office for every little thing, and the patients who had insurance had nothing holding them back either. Their reasoning was that they paid their premiums and wanted their money's worth. More testing was available and the new technology started to drive healthcare costs up further. Hospital costs were skyrocketing as well. I found it amazing that politicians and some segments of the public were so quick to try to blame doctors for the rise in healthcare costs. Ben had not raised his fees in five years, while the cost of living went up as did the cost of almost everything else needed to keep an office operating.

The years before the 1970s seemed to be the heyday of medicine. There were no middlemen to decide treatment or tell the doctor how to practice. Medicine was based strictly on the doctor/patient relationship, and doctors had more autonomy in their care of patients.

The first CAT scanner was invented in 1972 and was used commercially beginning in 1975. Technology was beginning to play a big part in diagnosis, and having a correct and fast diagnosis was crucial. In 1971, the MRI was invented, although it was not immediately used in patient diagnosis. Notwithstanding all diagnostic miracles of technology, it also contributed to driving health costs up. In the day, a doctor figured out what was wrong with a patient and tried to fix it without the constant threat of a lawsuit. There were suddenly more tests available used to diagnose medical problems and also used as a defensive measure against the rash of lawsuits that had begun to flourish. Up till that time, doctors could be sued only if they really messed up and only for real damages, not for the lottery.

Then came the HMOs (Health Maintenance Organizations). The groundwork had been laid for years, but in 1973, the U.S. Department of Health and Human Services passed the HMO Act, which cemented, in the United States, a new healthcare coverage that cost less than traditional insurance. There was, however, a limit on the scope of available treatments and payments. The HMO was able to offer cheaper health care by first, negotiating with physicians while providing them with large numbers of patients who had signed onto their program. Second, the HMO eliminated certain treatments that were felt to be unnecessary due to cost. Third, the HMO promised a focus on preventive care for patients, which didn't really happen.

It all sounded good for patients by offering low-cost health care, but there were so many restrictions that doctors in the program avoided referring patients at times, resulting in medical conditions becoming more serious. Apparently the doctors did this for economic reasons. A doctor was paid a fixed fee per patient each year. Each time a patient was referred to another doctor, the fee for that referral was deducted from the primary doctor's payment. Ben did not sign up when approached to do so because he could not afford to accept lower fees and higher numbers of patients. Both were nearly impossible for a solo physician, so he continued to be captain of his own ship and was happy doing it his way.

As part of Ben's occupational medicine practice, several industries in the area besides Johnson and Johnson, such as Mobil Oil Co., employed him for medical services. One of these was the New Jersey Garden State Highway Commission, where he did exams on new employees and took care of injured ones. When the Commission built an incredible outdoor arts center on the Parkway, Ben had the responsibility of being on call in case one of the performers needed medical care.

There were shows every week during the summer, and it was

great because he was needed at most of them. I was invited to go also, and we were given front row center seats. When Liberace came down with a sore throat before his performance, Ben had to spray and ease his throat pain so he could go on stage. When performers had any ailment, Ben had to tend to them, so it was a different and fun aspect of his practice. Once we took the boys to see a famous rock band, and they thought we were very hip. The sound system was so good and we sat so close, we may have been hip, but we also were deaf.

One Friday during office hours, I received a call from the Garden State Arts Center. Popular singer Andy Williams was in town to perform, but he wanted to play tennis that day. Knowing that Ben played tennis, the Center's manager, Mr. Lord, called to say, "We want Dr. K. to come right over so he can join Mr. Williams in a tennis match."

I was elated. Imagine a tennis match with a star! I put him on hold so I could tell Ben.

When I relayed the message, he responded with, "Are you kidding? I have patients to see. I can't just walk out on them."

"Are you out of your mind? I can cancel your patients and reschedule them." I countered. "This is a once-in-a-lifetime thing. You can't turn this down."

"What I can't do is desert my patients last minute. So tell Andy Williams I won't be able to play," he reiterated.

I was upset but I gave the message to Mr. Lord while I fumed inside. And Ben could possibly have won!

Chapter 11

The Messiah is coming! The Messiah is coming! That was the buzz around our neighborhood after the word got out that, ten years after our first child was born, when Scott was ten and Michael was nine, I was pregnant. In the '70s very few women age thirty-five and over were opting to get pregnant. If they did, the medical thinking was that something could go wrong and the baby might be born with defects. My pregnancy was thought of as a miracle, and I was accorded incredible attention and respect wherever I appeared. Kids in the neighborhood would ring our bell and ask if they could rub my protruding belly for good luck, and I let them. Everyone I knew was excited. We were a little less excited just thinking of going back to bottles, bibs, and cribs plus crying, burping, spitting, and pooping — the physical joys of parenthood. As the months crept by however, the idea of another cherub to love in the family, made us happy.

Actually, we could have opted out. In 1970, two years before I became pregnant, New York State passed the first abortion law of the land, and we did inquire about it. Apparently you had to prove one of several reasons to terminate a pregnancy. A woman could abort if in the first approximate three months (1) she was not mentally stable; (2) she was physically unable to carry to term; or (3) she was economically unable to care for the child. I guess having to give up my beautiful knit dresses for house dresses that could withstand spit-up was not a reason.

Since I did not pass on any level, we would be adding another little one to our family. Personally, I value life, but in my own mind, I struggled with the conflict of possibly making a decision to end a life and the freedom of having that choice. I do totally believe in a woman's right to choose and not have the government dictate what her choice should be. I joke about how the determination was made not to abort, but in my heart, I knew I could not terminate a life that I helped create.

Nine months sailed by and the big day arrived. Ben and Scott had gone off to the recycling plant with bags of bottles. In those days, if you were concerned about the environment, you had to save your glass and plastic bottles and take them to a local plant to be recycled. To encourage this, you were paid an amount per bottle, which was an incentive for having to drag all those bottles there in your car. There were always long lines, so the incentive worked for those who waited. Michael was left to watch over me with instructions to page Dad on his beeper if anything happened. Of course, within an hour of their leaving, my water broke and Michael could not rouse Ben on his beeper. He was getting pretty nervous, but I assured him we could call a taxi to get to the hospital.

We finally reached Ben, and when he got to a telephone and called me, he said with true medical decision making, "Cross your legs because we are next in line to dump these bottles, and we are not losing our turn in line."

So I did just that till Ben got home, and we raced away to the hospital. I was speedily prepped for delivery, and then the joke was on me.

"When do I get my spinal block of anesthesia?" I cried in desperation.

The attending nurse clearly answered, "You waited too long. This baby is coming now! Push!

"Well, I can push but how about breathing?" I wailed.

No answer, so I began to pant just like I saw being done in the movies. Natural childbirth was excruciatingly difficult, but it worked. A beautiful baby boy was born. Our Messiah had arrived! David was his name.

I was struggling with taking care of the children and spending more time helping Ben in the office. The insurance companies had many new rules and requirements, and a whole new set of codes had to be used if we wanted payment in a timely manner. In order to comply, I was now working in the office thirty hours a week, so we made the decision to hire someone to live in, do light housekeeping, and help with the children.

My sister-in-law Susan recommended an agency and before long they contacted me by phone. "We have a lovely lady from Haiti we would like you to interview. She is very sweet and proficient, but the only thing is, she doesn't speak English, only French. She's very willing to learn, and if you could help her and sponsor her, you will not regret the effort."

I thought I would take the chance and agreed to an interview the following day. In the meantime, I made tracks to the local bookstore and bought a pocket handbook of French words with English translations.

I prepped the boys by explaining, "My new helper, if I hire her, does not speak English, and you guys could really shine if, when you speak to her, you would point to what you need and repeat the word several times slowly. That's how she will learn English."

They thought of it as a neat game and agreed.

The next day the doorbell rang, and Protégé stood in our foyer, suitcase in hand, smiling with the kindest smile ever. She was a short, round, tan-skinned woman with wise eyes. I liked her immediately. Armed with my little blue dictionary, I welcomed her and introduced myself and the boys. After a few awkward questions (with both of us looking up words to translate), I attempted to tell her about the duties of the job, and she seemed to understand and cried when I told her she was hired. I hired her on my intuition alone, which was a lucky decision. When I asked the boys to show her to her room, Scott took her hand and led her into the kitchen.

"Protégé," he said, as he pointed to the unreachable top of a wooden hutch, "candy, candy." Again he repeated while pointing to my hiding place, "Candy, candy." Scott's Mom hadn't raised a fool.

Protégé was a blessing. She adored the children and was a pleasure to have in our home. I was able to spend lots of time in the office as more and more paperwork and administrative burdens were being forced on doctors. I didn't mind working because I enjoyed talking to the patients, and they seemed to like having what they thought was an insider's link to the doctor. I began to hear all their problems and turned a sympathetic ear to their sicknesses.

I agreed with Ben when one day he said, "You know, I believe most of the ailments that patients seek me out for are due to stress."

With that in mind, Ben very often approached medicine taking an unusual tack. The patients and I had to laugh when they sometimes came out of his office with prescriptions that read: "immediately take a vacation" or "you need to increase your sex life," or "be kind to each other, it will improve your heart," or "I'm watching you. Take your meds."

These were the years when practicing medicine was soooo

good for Ben. I watched my roommate come home from the office each night—eager, happy, and satisfied to be able to help people feel better. Being a caregiver is not an easy task, so for the life of me, I couldn't understand people who always complained that doctors make too much money. Given the fact that the cost of training to be a physician is out of sight, most doctors didn't make near enough to compensate them for what they accomplished every day. There were those docs who did make a lot of money, but they were usually specialists who had risky situations, such as surgeons or neurosurgeons. Many believed that physicians should be civil servants, like in other nations with socialized medicine. I would like to ask how that is working for them.

Chapter 12

With all our energy concentrating on Ben's career, the Vietnam War seemed to be on our minds less and less. The scenes on TV were still disturbing, as were the ongoing protests and rallies. Military personnel were coming home with crippling disabilities to a country that seemed not to care.

It was in 1973 when Ben heard that some of the prisoners of war had been released and were home. One of them, Colonel Fred Cherry, had been shot down on October 22, 1965. At the time, Colonel Cherry was piloting an F-105 with the 35th Tactical Fighter Squadron, which was Ben's squadron that he had been medically responsible for. Colonel Cherry spent seven years and four months in captivity, being released on February 12, 1973.

His story was compelling. Colonel Cherry was the first black officer captured by the North Vietnamese. Another captured officer, a young navy flier, was a southerner who was racist. Their captors put them into the same cell, thinking their attitude toward each other would help the Vietcong break them down. The prisoners were both in terrible physical shape and near death. But they endured, and their endurance helped them to overcome the worst kind of brutality. This bond saved their lives, and their story is a tribute to the strength and softness of the human spirit. Ben was ecstatic to hear of Colonel Cherry's return. He wrote the Colonel a long letter to express his faith in his return and his delight in having him home. Ben received the following letter dated May 1, 1973:

1 May 73

Dear Ben,

I may have been a permanent shut-in for the past seven and one-half years in the Hanoi Hilton, but the acuity of my memory was, and still is, and will continue to be in A-1 condition. And so it was especially appreciated to hear from another of my friends from Yokota days. Thank you so very much for taking the time to write me such a nice letter. I was surprised to learn of your military separation, but then life altered the service careers of many of my old Yokota friends during the time of my captivity. I trust your present position as medical director of a Johnson and Johnson affiliate plus your private practice have brought you success and challenge.

Culminating with my homecoming parade and banquet in Suffolk, Virginia, my activities have consisted of frantic rounds of speeches, school visits, documentary films, and travels up and down the East Coast to attend testimonial functions. If you get a chance, look through the TV Guide on August 10. ABC newsmen with their cameras rolling have tracked my path for the past few weeks obtaining footage for a POW documentary film on me which is scheduled for public release some time the second week in August. I'm certain you would find portions of the film quite interesting.

Though my long-range goals are yet in the hazy stage, my short-range plans are rather solid. I will be attending the National War College at Ft. McNair commencing this August. This program lasts for almost one year, following which I tentatively plan to continue my civilian academic pursuits. Of course, I intend to remain in the Air Force during these school days, perhaps under the Operation Bootstrap educational program. From then on, I'm not sure what I would like to do. Naturally I would love to get back into the cockpit once again, but, as you may know, my aircraft ejection injuries, complicated by retarded, primitive medical attention and torture while in prison will necessitate further surgery, and there is the strong possibility that I may not be able to fly again. Yet all this is in the future and I've learned the patient, hard way to simply take one day at a time.

So many of the people we both knew are in the Washington area or nearby bases—Jerry Hoblitt, Col. Peters, the Eftings, the list goes on and on. You would enjoy a visit to D. C. for a reunion with these people. I'll be living in the BOQ at Andrews until approximately late July, so if you have any free time or are on a business trip out this way, please write or give me a *call (leave a message with the desk answering service if I'm not there) at area 555-423-1412. Incidentally, I'm sure you are happy to know that Quincy Collins also made it out of the North in pretty good shape.*

Ben, again I want to thank you for writing to me, for remembering me and the life at Yokota. My fellow ex-POWs and I couldn't have endured the long, arduous, painful years without believing in our God, our country, the American people and particularly, knowing we kept the faith of our Air Force friends.

My best wishes to you, Fred Cherry.

The Vietnam War ended with the fall of Saigon on April 30, 1975. The Vietcong gained control of the city and all US personnel were evacuated. That morning, a North Vietnam tank appeared at Independence Palace, and a flag was raised above it. South Vietnam surrendered and Vietnam became a communist country. The war was over. Vietnam is under communist power to this day.

Chapter 13

The momentum of change in medicine had shifted into third gear. It was amazing how many third-party organizations started to have a say in how doctors practiced their profession. Medicaid had its rules and regulations as did Medicare and Blue Cross/Blue Shield. Private insurance companies would pick and choose what would be paid and what wouldn't be paid depending on how much profit they could make. Patients and doctors were caught in the middle. The new wave of HMOs began usurping patients from every doctor's practice that did not sign with them.

Almost daily, patients came into the office crying.

"What's the matter?" we asked at the front desk.

"I was just signed on to an HMO where I work," was the standard answer. "I must go to a doctor of their choosing."

This was a big blow to Ben. He had been taking care of these patients for several years.

There was a lot of industry in New Jersey, and he had groups of private patients from the surrounding workplaces whom he had contracted with for occupational medicine programs. Every week records of patients who were employed by the local bank or nearby Rutgers University were being transferred. Although his practice remained viable, Ben realized he was caught up in a tide of circumstances that he had no control over. It compared to big business taking the place of mom and pop stores.

Then there was the matter of cash flow. Insurance companies forced us to hire a person whose only job was just to do the complicated forms required to get paid. If there was only one small mistake on a form, it was sent back to us and that would delay payment sometimes for months. If the insurance company decided the code we used was not to their liking, it would be denied. Then the office had to argue with the company if we thought we were right.

When I hired an insurance person to do these forms, the first comment she made to me was, "I know how to deal with the insurance companies. I worked for one for five years. The first thing they taught me was how to use certain stall tactics to delay payment. After all, the longer the insurance company could keep their money and get paid interest on it, the happier and richer they were."

I became even more immersed in the business part of the practice because having a practice was really like running a small business. Ben wanted to just see his patients, do his own thing in medicine, and wanted no part of the business segment. So he evoked what I named the "turtle law." He pulled his head in and just let me run things.

In fact only once a year, right before tax time, would he ask me the inevitable question, "How much money did I make this year?" I would bring him up to snuff and tell him what portion the IRS was getting.

He would always respond with predictable angst, "Do you know out of a five-day work week, I work two days just for the US government?"

April 15th was never a good day.

Time was whooshing by like our kids on their roller skates. The boys were so much fun to raise. I don't ever remember them giving us one moment of grief. However, I do recall certain instances that made us a bit crazy. I recall an incident with Scott when he was disgruntled about a punishment he had received for hitting his brother. The phone rang and a colleague of Ben's who lived in the neighborhood said, "Bobbie, do you know that I just saw Scott a few blocks away, sitting on the curb with a red western-styled bandana in his lap. I stopped my car and asked him what he was doing and he said he was running away from home. 'I have all my stuff wrapped in this bandana and I'm waiting for a bus,' he told me."

The doctor ended with "I didn't want to let him know that no buses came into our development, but I'm calling to inform you about the runaway."

I was embarrassed, then furious, and stormed out the door and drove to the scene of the crime. Trying to appear nonchalant, I acted surprised to see my firstborn eight year old rejecting me and opting to run from our home.

He was sitting on the curb with his knapsack, sad blue eyes, and peach-cheeked angel-like face. All I wanted to do was tousle his blonde hair and hug him till he squealed. My heart ached.

"What are you doing here?" I naïvely asked, feeling very apprehensive.

"I'm waiting for a bus so I can run away from home," he nervously answered.

Trying to appear unconcerned, I informed him that no bus would come. I don't know what possessed me, but I guess I just wanted him to feel overwhelmed and to decide to come home. I told him I would drive him to the bus station in town if he really wanted to run away, all the time being fairly sure he would opt to be grateful to just get a ride home. I was wrong!

He jumped in the car and said, "OK."

Now I had to play out the scenario, sure he would back out at the station, which was five minutes away. But what if he didn't? My heart was pounding. What had I gotten myself into?

Much to my chagrin, when we pulled up to the station, he opened the door and started to get out. Then I became desperate. I lost it!

"Get in the car and close the door right now!" I screamed in sheer panic.

My screaming made him jump. Normally, I never screamed. He had an automatic reaction and quickly got back in the car. It had been a test of wills that had backfired. He was probably as scared as I was. How could I fix this?

When he was in, I drove away and switched to my usual calm and motherly voice, "Scott, honey, I just remembered, parents can't let their children just run away. They have to call the police to come and get them; otherwise, the parents could get into trouble. Let's go home, and you could sit on the front porch while I make the call."

I couldn't believe it, but he agreed. Scott sat himself stubbornly down on the porch while I went in the house to make my fake phone call to the police. But it was then that my mother's instinct and college-trained psychology kicked in. I appeared on the porch with a plate of home baked chocolate chip cookies (his favorite) and a cold glass of milk.

"I want you to have these before you go," I said, "but you know that Dad and I love you very much, and I'm sad that you want to leave us. Maybe you'll change your mind and we could work things out. But if not, whom should I give your tennis racket, basketball, football, new sneakers, and baseball cards to?"

Scott looked at me like a light had just been turned on in his head. He smiled, with that endearing smile of his.

"I've changed my mind." He got up, gave me a big hug and kiss, and went inside the house never to run away again!

Mike was our accident-waiting-to-happen child. One of our friends who was a general surgeon kidded that, from ages six to nine, he was Mike's personal surgeon. When kids in our backyard were throwing a rake up in a tree to try and get some seed pods to fall, the rake came down on Mike's lip and chin requiring twenty-three sutures and a visit to the surgeon. When Mike and a friend encountered an unfriendly dog, Mike was the one who had part of his earlobe bitten off. Of course, there was that visit to the surgeon.

When he was riding his friend's borrowed three-speed bicycle down our hill into the intersection while a car was approaching, he realized he did not know how to use the hand brakes. He tried to avert an accident, making a split-second decision as to whether he should turn off the road into a place where there were huge, jagged rocks, possibly sharp enough to split his head open, or risk pedaling into the intersection and getting hit by the car. He chose to ride into the intersection, grazing only the rear end of the car. He didn't get run over but did take a mean fall necessitating another trip to see the surgeon at the hospital. Over the years there were dozens of trips to the hospital. But, everyone told me he would outgrow this accident stage. Thank goodness they were right!

One day our little toddler David seemed very perplexed about something. He came to me and grabbed my hand, pulling and coaxing me to go with him. He was headed toward the master bathroom where he knew his daddy was. Ben was there shaving off his meticulously groomed beard he had grown after moving to New Jersey. David barged right into the bathroom, where Ben stood looking into the mirror at his now clean-shaven face. David stared at him in wide-eyed amazement.

Then he half hid himself behind me and shakily said, "Who dat, Mommy?"

I had to reintroduce two-year-old David to his daddy and explain to him about the shaving process. It took a while till David gave a relieved laugh and hugged his whisker-free buddy. For many years when David wanted to ignore something that Ben was telling him, he would laugh, point to his dad, and kiddingly say, "Who dat?"

Now Mike had his own way of dealing with us as parents. While he was being reprimanded about something, he would show his frustration by shaking, turning red in the face, pointing his finger, and pleading, "Don't speak!" Funny, many of our married friends adopted that same saying to silence their spouses.

Scott made it very simple. When he was asked or told to do something, he just merely disappeared! David had Scott and Mike, who made sure he did all the right things. He actually had to deal with what seemed like three fathers.

We took our job of raising children very seriously and gave it our all. When they were old enough to reason with, we taught them our rules. These were a few of them:

You never raise your hands or your voices to your mother or father.

There will be no allowances.

This is your home and everyone chips in to keep it going.

Everyone has a non-paying job.

In return, you will get what you need, within reason

You may never say "no" to your mother or father. Ever!

Of course, I was challenged on the last one by my future lawyers.

"What if you told us to go and stand on the roof?" my smart alecks questioned. "That's dangerous. We would have to say no."

"Well, that is where trust comes in," I answered. "Maybe the house was on fire, so I would tell you to get on the roof to save you. You see I would never tell or ask you to do anything that would harm you. So the rule stands. You do not have the option of saying no."

The rule was grudgingly accepted and is actually in force to this day, and the boys are grown men!

Chapter 14

It became disturbingly apparent that Ben was spending more time working harder than ever and spending less and less time with his family, especially me! His practice was fairly large and, combined with all his occupational medicine employment in industry, we found ourselves disconnected at times. I admit some of it was my fault. I was totally involved with the children, now ages twelve, eleven, and two and their activities. I entertained a lot for family, friends, and Ben's medical colleagues. I was also immersed in all sorts of civic, religious, medical, and charitable organizations. These were the activities expected of a good doctor's wife. The eyes of the community were focused not only on Ben but on the children and myself as well. I constantly reminded the older boys that they lived in a community fishbowl, and it was too bad, but they had better not do anything to embarrass us or I would have to kill them.

It wasn't unusual for me to be president or board member of several organizations at a time. My husband also became engaged in political issues and medical associations as well as continuing medical education. We were busy being busy, never noticing that we were unintentionally moving in our own individual directions. The children benefited, the community benefited, but we were becoming distant and singular where we used to be close and attached. We needed to stop and reconnect. We needed a vacation!

That's exactly what Ben would prescribe for his patients, so I begged him to prescribe it for us. Happily, he took the clue and planned a two-week getaway for us with some friends during the summer of '75. Grandma Lily and Grandpa Al came to stay at our house, and the kids were signed up for day camp.

Ben and I were soon joyfully on our way. Ah, no patients to worry about for two whole weeks. We couldn't wait. After a long airplane ride from La Guardia Airport in New York to Madrid, Spain, we boarded a private jitney-style bus to tour the captivating and charming countries of Spain, Portugal, and Morocco. We toured with our friends and a small group of five other pleasant couples. However, one couple had to interrupt their tour and be sent on ahead to the departure city to await the rest of the group. The reason was that this older man had suffered a heart attack before joining the tour and mistakenly thought he could continue on while constantly being short of breath. He hounded Ben every day, without end, about his health issues. Unfortunately, Ben was a captive ear.

Dr. K., as he was called by the tour guide because he had seen "MD" on the tour manifest, was asked to evaluate this man as a patient and determine his ability to continue to travel. Ben decided that he couldn't go on, so the man opted not to fly home, but be sent back to relax at a hotel with his wife and wait for the group. Ben, trying to be a Good Samaritan, was a bit annoyed but prescribed medication to get him through.

Our destinations in Spain included all the unique and seductive cities of Madrid, Toledo, Barcelona, Granada, Costa del Sol, Cordoba, and Seville. Succulent Spanish cooking aromas tweaked our senses at every stop. The Alhambra, an ancient Moorish palace, was magical and the gold-domed mosques were mystical wonders. The fiery passion of flamenco dancing enchanted us, but the cruelty of the bull fights rankled us.

Sometimes we drove one hundred miles or more on our tours, and all we could see was nothing more than acres and acres of parched land with rows and rows of olive trees. This proved to be a total problem on one of our day tours.

Before we started out, our guide warned us (the ladies in particular), "Now, there is no bathroom on our bus so make sure you use one before we leave. We'll be on the road for 180 miles."

We all complied, including all twelve females, and anticipated a day of interesting sightseeing. After about an hour and a half on the road, the inevitable happened! I had to go to the bathroom.

"Ben, what should I do? I have to go," I wailed.

"Well, just cross your legs, and I'll go to the front of the bus and ask our guide to stop at the nearest place," Ben offered.

He went to the front. When he came back, he passed on the information that we had at least another two hours to travel through stretches of olive groves, and there were no rest stops. I thought I was going to implode. We were on a two-lane highway with no shoulder, so I couldn't even get the driver to stop so I could use

Mother Nature as a refuge.

"Ben, I'm in pain," I pleaded. "I feel like I'm burning up, and I have the chills. Can't you do something?"

Ben, realizing that we now had a medical problem, went to the front of the bus to try to get the driver to stop somewhere. I could just squat behind an olive tree, anything to relieve a full bladder before it burst, I passed out, or I died! No go! I was getting ill, and there was nothing that was being done. I was about to become the "queen of mean" and yell and pound the seat, but just then the tour guide gave the driver instructions to pull into a long driveway of a solitary, dilapidated house.

He jumped off the bus and went inside, coming back in a few minutes to hasten me off the bus saying, "I just gave the woman of the house money to let you use the bathroom."

I bounded from my seat, made a marathon run into the farmhouse, and was told in Spanish by a sweet little old lady that the bathroom was at the top of the stairs. Leaping up the stairs two by two, I came face to face with an astonished old man in his pajamas who stared at me with a dazed and bewildered look. I'm sure he was wondering what a strange woman was doing upstairs in his house, heading for the same place he was. I regretfully brushed past him with a weak smile and a gracias and basically slammed this man's own bathroom door right in his face. I felt bad, but I was desperate.

Within moments I came back to the world of the living and came out of the bathroom to see this adorable little man still standing there in complete shock. As I headed toward the stairs feeling guilty and walking with my head down to avoid the man's evil eye, I looked up long enough to see eleven women waiting in line on the stairs, with the line stretching all the way to the door and outside.

We finished our tour in Spain and were so happy to experience Spain in all its glory.

We then took a choppy, ferry ride across the legendary Straits of Gibraltar to Morocco. It was there that I saw, for the first time, women wearing burkas. I was horrified and sad for them. They saw their whole world from a small net portal opening around the eyes. It bothered me a lot!

The sights in old Morocco were stunning. We haggled in the many dirty, crowded, unique bazaars, and when our suitcases were overflowing with treasures, we headed to Portugal.

Portugal was spectacular in a simpler way. It was made up of lots of little folksy towns. We traveled to most of them, and then made our way to the religious and special town of Fatima, where a miracle witnessed by three children was claimed to have happened.

Although it did not represent my beliefs, I chose to walk around the shrine of Fatima on my knees, as others who were believers, were doing. I was deeply moved by the spirituality of the moment although my knees were bruised and killing me! We were all quite despondent to leave this rare part of the world.

After an enchanting and romantic two weeks, we found ourselves at the airport for our return flight. It had been a trip designed to refresh us, and it really worked.

As we waited to board, the heart attack man approached Ben. "I am really not feeling up to par. If you write me a note to sit in first class, they will let me, and I would be much more comfortable given the circumstance."

He coaxed and coaxed till Ben and the flight crew were persuaded. The patient was sent to first class, and we finally were boarded in coach class.

When we were in the air at last and settled down, Ben called the stewardess. "I'm a physician and have a patient in first class who I need to check on."

"Oh," she cautioned, "I can't let you go up there. That's first class and you aren't permitted."

"But he's my patient and I would like to see him," Ben answered, slowly rising out of his seat.

"I'm sorry, sir, you cannot go beyond the curtain." she retorted.

So Ben shrugged and sat back down and began his nap. One nap and two meals later for both of us, we were just about fifty miles from landing at La Guardia Airport when a stewardess hurriedly came to our seats.

"Are you a doctor?" Ben confirmed, and the stewardess cried, "We need your help! A young man seems to be having a medical problem and is on the floor in first class. We don't know what's wrong with him. Would you come and see him?"

Ben made no effort to get up, but in a slow and deliberate voice and manner said, "I am so sorry that I cannot help, but I am not permitted in first class."

"But we need you," she said desperately. "We'll be in a holding flight pattern for the next forty minutes, but if this man is ill, we can request permission to land immediately."

Now came the dilemma, but Ben grabbed the opportunity to go to first class, check the man on the floor, and check his own patient as well. The man on the floor was just drunk, but his patient was having chest pain. Ben tended to both of them and made the decision that the plane should land as soon as possible, which the pilot did with great relief. Once on the ground, there were ambulances and special escorts to get the patients quickly through the arrival gates and customs. As Ben started to disembark with his patients and myself, he was stopped.

"Oh no," the guard said, "You have to go in line with all the rest of the passengers."

After all the hassle, with no thank-you from anyone, and standing in line for an hour to get through customs, Ben made a decision. "You know, I will NEVER use MD with my name again when I travel and NEVER volunteer my services. NEVER!" Silly man, he should have known there was never a never!

After we arrived home, we made a pact to take two vacations a year. Alone! So, the next summer found Mr. and Mrs. instead of Dr. and Mrs. on their way to visit Athens and to cruise the Greek islands on a small private boat. Athens, the birthplace of western civilization is the capitol of Greece. It's a sprawling city, rich in history and antiquities. We were surprised to see that the Acropolis, built to honor the Goddess Athena and the Temple of Zeus, which housed the first Olympic Games of 1896, were mixed right in with ordinary, dingy, city buildings.

We enjoyed our sightseeing and then set out to find Dr. Panadous, who was Ben's colleague, and had the same medical position with Mobil Oil in Athens as Ben did in New Jersey. We found him and his wife at home and were invited for a drink. When we entered their villa, we were speechless. The doctor's wife, Rose was an archeologist with the National Museum, and one whole room held treasures of coins, gold and silver, and pottery, which she and her team had excavated. She kept her amazing discoveries in floor-to-ceiling glass cases and explained that the Greek government allowed her to keep a percentage of her findings. We thought we were in a museum and were quite overwhelmed.

This lovely couple took us under their wings and showed us the local side of Athens. Unbelievable! On our last night in Athens, before boarding our cruise boat, we were taken to dinner in quaint Piraeus, an ancient port of Athens. Six other executives and their wives from Mobil met us there at an exclusive seafood restaurant, where we were seated at a long, dark wooden table right on the beach and treated to outstanding personal service. The view of the blue Mediterranean was stunning, and we watched the brilliant, red sunset act as a background for the tired fishing boats that pulled right up close to us on the grey colored sand.

The chef picked a fish right off one of the boats, placed it on an open, blazing fire, covered it with exotic herbs, and then brought it right to our table. The fish was as long as our table and it was cut down the middle with the rough-skinned flaps pulled back. We each helped ourselves to this fresher than fresh, sweet as sugar fish, along with every roasted vegetable ever grown, and began our feast. The wine flowed and we were in epicurean heaven.

Then it happened. One of the doctors, who was from France, turned to his wife and said, "Tushy, would you please pass the salt?"

I thought the wine had gotten to me or I was hearing things.

He repeated, "Tushy, the salt, if you don't mind."

Well, I was ready to crack up. The word "tushy" is fairly well known and used as the vernacular of buttocks, butt, or derriere.

This proper French gentleman was sitting there calling his wife an ass, over and over again. Ben and I locked glances and almost choked on our food.

I turned to Tushy and said, "Oh, is that your name?"

"Yes," she replied. "My real name is Isabel, but I prefer my middle name of Tushy."

Well, the rest of the meal was fun, due more to our French table companions than anything. When the evening was over, we returned to our hotel after saying our good-byes. We could only make it to the lobby before we burst out laughing till the tears flowed. It was a memorable evening, indeed.

I have never found the right words to totally describe the beauty of the western Greek islands. I don't think there was a name for the color of the blue water surrounding all the islands. The hue of the water was a combination of turquoise, sapphire, aquamarine, teal, and azure blue. The water sparkled like a precious gem, hypnotizing my eyes as I gazed across miles of calmness with only a few interruptions from a white-capped wave. When we docked at our first island port, the love affair began for me. Not too many cruises came to this small island because the cruise ships were too big. Our boat was just right.

When we disembarked, we were met by colorfully clothed townspeople with arms full of flowers. It was a sight to see! Then our group walked two blocks to a charming taverna to taste all the Greek specialty foods and wash it down with ouzo. Ouzo is an anise-flavored aperitif, a symbol of Greek culture. It could knock you out!

There was a local, noisy, amateur three-piece band, in Greek costumes playing during dinner. When we all realized we had lingered too long and our boat was leaving port shortly, we emptied out onto the street. The musicians followed us out of the taverna continuing to play. What a sight! What fun! We danced in the streets the entire way to the boat. The townspeople were dancing with us and kissing us good-bye, making it seem like we were part of a movie set. It was one of the loveliest moments of any trip we had ever taken. I shall always be in love with the Greek islands!

The scenery on our cruise took my breath away, and I didn't get it back till our jet took off from Athens to the United States.

On our third night out, standing at the over-polished mahogany rail with Ben's arm around me and a perfect pink sunset in our view, I quickly fell into a mushy mood.

"It takes my breath away," I said out loud.

"I am enjoying it so much," the woman standing next to us said, "but I'm afraid my husband is in too much pain to fully appreciate where we are."

So stupid me asked, wondering what he was doing on a cruise, anyway, with so much pain. "Oh, what's the matter? Is it serious?"

"Well, we had an auto accident days before our trip and he injured his back and leg. He's mistakenly left his meds at home, and his back is killing him."

"So sorry," I mumbled. My mellow mood was broken, and I knew right away what was going through Ben's head.

We always traveled with our medical kit packed in a suitcase that had medications for just about any malady that might occur. I said nothing and Ben said nothing.

We then made pleasant chitchat, but when they said good night and the man started to walk away bent over and with a limp, Ben called out, "Listen, I'm a physician and might have some medication that will help for the days of the cruise. I have some anti-inflammatory and mild pain meds I could give you, but I'll need to take a history and examine you first. If you want, I could come to your cabin in a little while, examine you, and give you the meds. I have only one request. Do not tell anyone on the boat that I am a doctor."

They agreed, and within the hour, this new patient found relief.

"I knew you would do that," I said when we were back in our cabin.

"It's the nature of the beast," was his answer, and we quickly fell sound asleep in a stupor brought on by a soothing, swaying boat.

Someone broke the calm by banging on our cabin door at seven in the morning. Ben jumped out of bed like a jackrabbit to unlock the door. "What the hell is this?" What he saw, and I didn't, was a line of seven people waiting in the hallway.

The first in line said, "We discovered that you were a doctor, and we all need some help or advice while we are at sea. Could you help us?"

Someone had squealed! No surprise, Ben was soon tagged as personal physician to the passengers for the rest of the cruise.

"Well, I might as well go back to using doctor and dropping mister. The mister handle just didn't seem to work," Ben announced at the end of our cruise.

However, from that vacation forward, almost always on our vacations there were times when someone needed care or advice. I was right, there's never a "never." But, then again, there's never an "always."

Ben repeated that scenario time after time on all our trips as we became hopelessly addicted to traveling. In our years together, we managed to enjoy sixteen cruises and visits to forty-six countries and thirty-six states. He had the privilege of helping patients all over the world.

Chapter 15

For years I watched him fight on the battlefield of life and death. Every day was a private war with sickness and dying; he was determined to be the victor. Sometimes his determination stemmed from his medical training and the responsibility of upholding the Hippocratic Oath—sometimes it was just his ego not wanting to lose. Mostly, this was about having the ability and the power to make another person feel better, to cure disease, and to save or prolong life.

No wonder people accuse doctors of acting like God. In truth, they are thrown into an arena with all sorts of problems and called on to solve them in a God-like manner. Being humble in the process is a feat all its own.

In the sixth century BC, medicine adopted the Hippocratic Oath, one of the oldest binding documents in history, as its own. The Oath of Hippocrates is widely believed to have been written as a Greek medical text by Hippocrates, the so-called father of medicine, who lived in the fifth century BC. It required a physician to swear upon a number of healing gods that he would uphold certain ethical standards. I remember when Ben's medical school class repeated out loud this classic version of the Hippocratic Oath in unison at graduation.

The original oath, translated into English is as follows:

I swear by Apollo, the healer, Asclepius, Hygieia, and Panacea and I take witness all the gods, all the goddesses, to keep according to my ability and my judgment, the following Oath and agreement:

To consider dear to me, as my parents, him who taught me this art; to live in common with him and, if necessary, to share my goods with him; To look upon his children as my own brothers, to teach them this art; and that by my teaching, I will impart a knowledge of this to my own sons, and to my teacher's sons, and to disciples bound by an indenture and oath according to the medical laws, and no others.

I will prescribe regimens for the good of my patients according to my ability and my judgment and never do harm to anyone.

I will give no deadly medicine to any one if asked, nor suggest any such counsel; and similarly I will not give a woman a pessary to cause an abortion.

But I will preserve the purity of my life and my arts.

I will not cut for stone, even for patients in whom the disease is manifest; I will leave this operation to be performed by practitioners, specialists in this art.

In every house where I come I will enter only for the good of my patients, keeping myself far from all intentional ill-doing and all seduction and especially from the pleasures of love with women or with men, be they free or slaves.

All that may come to my knowledge in the exercise of my profession or in daily commerce with men, which ought not to be spread abroad, I will keep secret and will never reveal.

If I keep this oath faithfully, may I enjoy my life and practice my art, respected by all humanity and in all times; but if I swerve from it or violate it may the reverse be my life.

Ben told me he was scared and proud as he recited the oath — scared of the responsibilities he was swearing to and scared of leaving the rigorous yet comfortable womb of education. It was an awesome undertaking. At the time, I believe most of the doctors felt very proud and privileged to be required to uphold certain ethical standards. It was an expression of ideal conduct for physicians.

The fact that the classic version required a physician to swear upon a number of healing gods did not sit well as time went on. So, in 1964 a modern version of the traditional oath was penned by Dr. Louis Lasagna, Academic Dean of the School of Medicine at Tufts University. It's a fact now, that not all medical schools require their graduating doctors to take the Hippocratic Oath. But it's as important now, as ever, for doctors to have an agreed statement of ethical principles.

On the other hand, the realities of the modern world seem too complex now to be covered by a simplistic oath. With huge scientific changes unheard of in Hippocrates' time, how can a physician swear to a single oath?

Most medical schools administer some form of oath. However, a physician is not required to take an oath. The modern version is seen as having little value beyond that of upholding tradition. Only the person taking the oath can judge if the swearing to the modern version has any importance:

> *I swear to fulfill, to the best of my ability and judgment, this covenant:*
>
> *I will respect the hard-won scientific gains of those physicians in whose steps I walk. And gladly share such knowledge as is mine with those who are to follow.*
>
> *I will apply, for the benefit of the sick, all measures that are required, avoiding those twin traps of overtreatment and therapeutic nihilism.*
>
> *I will remember that there is art to medicine as well as science and that warmth, sympathy, and understanding may outweigh the surgeon's knife or the chemist's drug.*
>
> *I will not be ashamed to say "I know not," nor will I fail to call in my colleagues when the skills of another are needed for a patient's recovery.*
>
> *I will respect the privacy of my patients, for their problems are not disclosed to me that the world may know. Most especially must I tread with care in matters of life and death. If it is given to me to save a life, all thanks. But it may also be within my power to take a life; this awesome responsibility must be faced with great humbleness and awareness of my own frailty. I must not play at God.*
>
> *I will remember that I do not treat a fever chart, a cancerous growth, but a sick human being whose illness may affect the person's family and economic stability. My responsibility includes these related problems, if I am to care adequately for the sick.*
>
> *I will prevent disease whenever I can, for prevention is preferable to cure.*
>
> *I will remember that I remain a member of society with special obligations to all my fellow human beings, those sound of mind and body as well as the infirm.*
>
> *If I do not violate this oath, may I enjoy life and art, be respected while I live and remembered with affection thereafter.*
>
> *May I always act so as to preserve the finest traditions of*

my calling and may I long experience the joy of healing those who seek my help.

Ben absorbed and took his pledge very seriously. I always thought of him as a cross between Sherlock Holmes and Don Quixote, and I couldn't have been more proud of the physician he had become!

Chapter 16

Many physicians who lived and practiced in our part of New Jersey were an overflow of those who lived or trained in New York or Philadelphia. When relocating to New Jersey, they brought with them the latest technology and savvy of cosmopolitan hospitals and medical schools. Relocated patients also had the advantage of advanced medicine and demanded the best from their doctors. In the '70s, two medical schools merged in our area and became the College of Medicine and Dentistry of New Jersey, with the campus practically in our backyard. Also, nearby was Johnson and Johnson, a very well-respected pharmaceutical company. So the bar had been raised for good medicine in our part of the state.

As one of the medical directors of Johnson and Johnson, Ben experienced firsthand the wonderful health programs they had in place for their employees. They were always ahead of the curve. He chose to emulate those programs in his private practice saying, "If it's good enough for Johnson and Johnson then it's good enough for my own patients."

Preventive medicine, which was his driving force, was becoming part of medicine's new sophistication, being imported from the cities into the suburbs. New patients quickly found their way to the office when they became aware of Ben's philosophy. Patients were becoming tougher about what they wanted, and that included all the latest tests and medications. It was becoming a real challenge to satisfy many of them. In the meantime, an evil force was at work. The New Jersey county that we lived in was reported to have an unusually high cancer rate. Ben was diagnosing and fighting more cancer cases in his practice, and because of the formidable nature of the disease, cancer seemed to be winning.

Losing patients this way was a terrible blow to Ben. He became involved, through his occupational medicine contacts, in the movement to stop the big industries in the area from dumping into the Raritan River, which surrounded many communities in central New Jersey. This dumping in the water was thought to be a contributing factor in the possible cause of cancer. The problem was that when the EPA caught the offending company and fined it, the company paid the fine and went right back to dumping. It was a vicious circle that didn't get resolved till years later when the damage was already done.

At that period of time (in the '70s), another demon started to claim people left and right. Ben's own father, David succumbed to lung cancer from smoking, and it hit home hard.

"How can I get my patients who smoke to stop?" Ben agonized to me one day during a lunch break.

"Well, we give out lots of booklets provided to us by the Cancer Society, and you certainly include histories and chest X-rays on your exams," I explained. "What more could you be doing?"

He thought and then answered, "There's a machine called a spirometer, which measures air flow in the lungs, used to diagnose COPD (Chronic Obstructive Pulmonary Disease). Perhaps if I included this test, I could show a smoker how breathing is affected and diminished by smoking and give him the incentive to quit before it's too late. Also, there seems to be a great deal of upper respiratory problems in the population of New Jersey."

Shortly afterward, spirometer testing was started in the office, and after a year of patient tracking, we had twenty-four patients who quit smoking. Ben was not winning the war but won a few battles for sure. One of the battles he unfortunately lost hit quite close to home. We had neighbors, Jim and Anne, living across the street from us, who were a sweet couple from Yugoslavia. They were patients of Ben's and also became friends. We were invited to their parties and we invited them to ours. On one occasion I had an outdoor party in the fall with golden wheat sheaves as decorations on the tables and colorful leaves sprinkled all over fat pumpkins and odd-shaped gourds. When Jim and Anne arrived, I greeted them and saw that Jim had tears in his eyes.

It scared me, and I asked, "Are you all right?" Jim openly volunteered that he had been politically active in his country and had had a tough life. They just narrowly escaped the Nazis to go underground and get to the United States with their three children.

"So why are you crying?" I asked.

"Because this scene, here in your backyard, reminds me of fall and farmers' harvest time in my country. As you traveled the countryside, you could see all the gathered, gold wheat and yellow-orange pumpkins. They were like flecks on the landscape, and my memory brings it all back to me as I stand in your yard. I feel sad but happy to be here remembering."

Jim was a gentle giant of a man, and we were very stirred by his story. When he showed up soon afterward on a Sunday morning at our house complaining of shortness of breath, we were concerned. Ben opened the office and examined him, did an EKG, and assured him it was not his heart. When Ben did a spirometer test, he was alarmed. Jim was a patient who refused to have his yearly complete physical exam and rarely came to the office. He was also a smoker.

The next sequence of events took him to the emergency room and a chest X-ray which showed that one of his lungs was riddled with cancer. A thoracic surgeon was called in, and part of his lung was removed. He struggled through radiation and chemotherapy and then was told by Ben that he was to be seen in the office every month with no exceptions. Ben monitored Jim very closely and told him that he didn't escape the Nazis only to have cancer get him so soon. He survived seven years till this insidious disease claimed him, doing what the Nazis could not.

These series of events seemed to be taking a toll on Ben, who gained his pride from keeping people healthy. I found Ben alone on one particular, gloomy, rainy day, sitting in the den, kind of in a fugue.

"What's going on?" I inquired. "You look so morose."

He confided that he was really feeling down. "Do you think I make much of a difference in what I do? Do I really help anyone? I'm not convinced that I make much of an impact in people's lives. I used to feel I was a professional, really helping society, now I think I just function to fulfill insurance parameters and deliver government mandated entitlements. It used to be that people didn't expect medicine to fix every aspect of their lives. Now they go to the doctor for everything: feeling sad, being fat, whatever! I used to write in a patient's chart to remind myself what was going on, not so insurance companies could code my work and decide if I should get paid or not. I don't think doctors get the respect they deserve anymore."

"Wow, sounds like a pity party to me," I jumped in. "But you know what? You really make me mad and here's why. I figure that in my lifetime I may have the opportunity to help perhaps a dozen people, maybe. I mean really help and make a difference if I'm lucky. Now, in your lifetime, and think about it, you probably have had the advantage of helping thousands. Yes, that's right. If I do the math, you see approximately five thousand patients a year. Even if you only improve the health and lives of half of these patients, you are benefiting thousands of people each year. Thousands! That has an impact! I'm envious and angry that you don't see it."

Ben looked at me long and hard, then broke out in a satisfying grin.

"Well, you're right as usual. I guess I just wasn't thinking. I won't mention it again. Thanks." He got up from slumping in his chair with his face brightened. "Want a cup of coffee? We could talk more about my achievements."

Chapter 17

After living in New Jersey for more than a dozen years, we were living what I thought was a happy and blessed life. It was darn near perfect. Ben seemed to be enjoying his smooth-running practice and his grateful patients, and I truly believed all was well. But I wonder now if you ever really know another person's compass even if you are married to him. It puzzled me that in the midst of our ideal life, I was picking up vibrations of my loving mate's discontent.

I walked in on the good doctor on a Saturday morning sitting in his oversized chair, gazing out the window into our lush, green, manicured, suburban backyard. I had come into the office to retrieve my favorite coffee cup which I had left behind. It was very unusual to see him just sitting and staring into the space of the yard. Something was not right.

I startled him when I called out, "Hey, what are you doing here? Have some catching up to do? I don't see any paperwork."

He slowly swiveled his chair around and I didn't like the look in those intense hazel eyes now staring directly at me. He was deep in thought.

"I bet you were sitting here trying to think of where we would travel to on our next vacation."

"No," he revealed, "I was sitting here thinking of where I will be traveling to on the rest of my life's journey."

"Uh-oh," I said, "Do I see a midlife crisis about to happen?"

He responded with a denial but went on to say, "There is so little fulfillment for me anymore in my practice. Every day seems the same." His eyes were teary. "You see I really love just helping people and making a difference in their lives. But with all the extra burdens in medicine, it's overwhelming. Maybe solo practice is too demanding and I would do better with a medical group or partner. I don't know. Or maybe practicing in a more rural or underserved area would bring me back to the medicine I loved in the first place and help me keep it alive. What do you think?"

I heard his frustration loud and clear.

"I think I'll do whatever you want to do," I affirmed. "You know, the real challenge is to be yourself in a world that is trying to make you like everyone else. If you feel you would be more productive and happier in a different setting, then let's find the setting. As long as you aren't thinking of a third world country, I'm in!"

"But you're so content here. You have all your friends around you — you're happy."

"Listen," I said, "I can be happy anywhere. It's not about where you live; it's about a state of mind. I've always kept my old friends and made new ones. That will be the easy part and I've learned to pack and move like a pro." I added, "Take your time, think things over. We'll figure it out."

I was hoping the Saturday morning encounter would pass and be forgotten, but it didn't happen that way. By the next week, Ben had already begun his search. Now several search firms were calling a few times a day with offers and locations for a possible relocation. Most of the offers were out West, which really didn't appeal to us, or the Appalachia area which was not a place for our family. After months of overtures and offers, we heard of a doctor in southern Delaware who was looking for a partner. The area where he practiced Family Medicine was quite rural, but there were several industries nearby that were looking for a medical director. One of them made space suits for NASA's program, and this seemed quite enticing and fitting for Ben's Air Force experience and occupational medicine background.

Ben's colleagues thought he was crazy! "You want to leave sophisticated suburban New Jersey medicine and bury yourself in an area that is about five years behind in updated medicine?" they were all asking.

Undaunted, we traveled to Delaware to meet Dr. Morrow and see where he practiced. We were already familiar with parts of Delaware, since we had been stationed at Dover Air Force Base, but had really never traveled south of Dover other than to go to the beach. We rode just about half an hour south of Dover to Milford, a different world. We saw acres of farmland and chicken coops in between sleepy, little, old-fashioned towns. This was really rural America.

We met Dr. Morrow at his quaint office and were shown around. It seemed clean, basic, and functional. Our present office, with the touches I had added, was so much nicer, but this was a different setting and would be fine. We then toured the small, quiet, slow-paced hospital. It was certainly not equipped like the two big, busy hospitals Ben worked in, but it was appealing in a relaxed kind of way.

Having lunch with Dr. Morrow was very pleasant, and the conversation centered on how Ben might fit into and contribute to the doctor's practice. He was very laid-back and a contrast to Ben's vim and vigor; this might be a good match. They decided on a contract, which needed to be drawn up, and a start date. It all seemed to feel right although I was beginning to have doubts about everything being done so fast. I was getting a nervous stomach about lower Delaware referred to as "slower Delaware." I wondered if I should be concerned. On the ride home we were talking a blue streak. Ben was very upbeat. I was a bit more dubious. Should we do this or shouldn't we? The same feelings cropped up as they had when we left the Air Force to settle in New Jersey, and it was all centered on fear!

The fallout from our decision was terrible and toxic for our kids. The two older ones were in high school, and the little one was in kindergarten. A move was going to be tough for Scott and Mike, who were doing very well in the higher grades. They had a hissy fit.

"How could you do this to us?" they wailed.

I tried to reassure and comfort them but was getting nowhere fast. What a dilemma. Ben and I chose to make the change quite fast, hoping to shorten the pain. A one-year contract was signed. My wonderful, beautiful home was put on the market. The practice was sold to a friend, and all the patients were notified. Ben would stay on for a month.

It was agony. Patients were calling and writing, upset that the doctor they had relied on for so long would not be there for them. One of Ben's patients was a reporter for the local newspaper and wrote a lovely article in the Sunday edition about Dr. K. and his caring for the community. I cried for the entire day. What were we doing?

Ben went to Delaware to begin practicing with Dr. Morrow and found an apartment on a beach close to the office. We stayed behind to sell the house in the summer of '76, hoping it would sell fast so we could purchase another one and have the children start school in the fall. I actually sold the house in three days by myself, but the buyers could not take ownership till after the first of the year. So the plan was to stay in New Jersey till winter vacation and make the transition halfway through the school year.

Ben was working and house hunting but coming home only every other weekend when he wasn't on call. As winter vacation approached, we wanted to spend some holiday time together, so we decided to go to the apartment on the beach for a long weekend. Ben gave me directions to the apartment and when I saw where it was, I gasped. He was way out in the boonies on a desolate stretch of sand called Slaughter Beach. What I couldn't know was that the name of that area was a foreshadowing of things to come.

Chapter 18

The night we traveled to Delaware, so we could spend some time with Ben, was horrific. Once we turned off the main highway, I realized we were riding in total darkness, surrounded by a milky grey fog. There were no street lights, and a dim, full moon gave off the only real light other than my headlights. I could only see several yards of gravel road ahead of me as the car crawled to the beach. Going over the narrow, creaky, unstable bridge from the mainland was terrifying. When we came to a dead end, almost two miles on the other side, I freaked out. I was so lost! I had been smart enough to bring my CB radio and in a "trying to be calm" voice, I attempted to rouse Ben so he could lead me to where he was. We had been using our CB radios on long car trips and even had our own "handles" as truck drivers called them—mine was "earth angel" and Ben's (believe it or not) was "rigor mortis."

Using my CB lingo I cried into my radio, "Breaker nine, breaker nine, this is earth angel for rigor mortis. Come in." No response. I repeated my plea, telling him where I was. Still, no answer.

Then, a welcome, familiar voice answered, "You must have passed the slight turn as you came off the bridge. That road will take you to the beach."

"Not if we don't get slaughtered first,...on Slaughter Beach. Get it?" I quipped.

We made it to the beach in time for Ben to get called into the hospital, as he was on call. The boys were very upset, but he had to go. Two patients had tried to commit suicide. It's strange, but it seems the emergency rooms usually get several attempted suicides every time there is a full moon. It's a fact!

We enjoyed the extra-long weekend that we spent on Slaughter Beach. During the day we looked at houses in the area. Surprisingly, we found a lovely, traditional, brick ranch house on a cul-de-sac 'led in an acre of trees. There was not a blade of grass in sight. ~all stream running through the backyard and a dock though the house was not in the town where the office was located, Milford was a short commute away. The house was in the district of one of the top five high schools in the country.

The house had been built by a local builder for himself and had all the best details and features. There were hand-planked wood floors, three fireplaces, a brick foyer and pecky cypress beams and paneling in the family room. A screened-in porch as well as a finished basement ran the length of the house. It was love at first sight! When our bid on the house was accepted, we were ecstatic.

We left Slaughter Beach, joyful and looking forward to the future, to start the packing process in New Jersey. By mid-February 1977, we were unpacked and settled in our new home in Delaware. Ben seemed to like his new position and the slow-paced hospital. We were welcomed into our new neighborhood and felt very comfortable with the friendly families on our block. David assimilated into kindergarten very nicely. Starting out at a strange high school was a different story for Scott and Mike. It was a bit tough on the older boys, but it didn't take long before a bevy of young people were knocking on our door looking for them.

They did have a small problem at the start. It was a predicament that we discussed at the dinner table one evening.

"You know, we really don't fit in here." Scott and Mike remarked.

"What do you mean?" I asked.

"Well, there are like two different groups in our school. There are the jocks and the heads," they explained. "We don't fit into either one. We like sports and play basketball and tennis, but are not really jocks. We're not heads because we aren't involved with pot, and so are not potheads. So we're kind of just out there, not fitting."

"Oh, I'm sure there are other kids that don't fit into either category," I responded. "Why don't you search them out?"

So that's exactly what the boys did and gathered and bonded with a great group of their own, enabling them to sail through high school enjoying it all. Many of these gals and guys still keep in touch.

It wasn't long before I became active in several interesting community clubs and medical groups. Our social life started to include nice couples who seemed to care about us even though we were told several times that it took about five years before you were considered a true "Delawarean." But we were certainly trying hard to fit into our new life.

We felt it to be a compliment when we were finally invited to our first Saturday night cocktail party at another physician's house. I donned my favorite chic, pink ultra-suede suit that was a Chanel design. I paired it with a simple, white silk blouse. I was feeling super confident! Ben wore his traditional navy blue blazer and khakis with a button down blue shirt and striped tie. He looked very Joe College. It was our first big social event since moving to Delaware. Even though we had attended dozens of incredible social events in the past, this one was of special importance to us. We so wanted to fit in.

Imagine our surprise upon entering the home of the party and realizing we were both very over-dressed. I couldn't remember when I felt more uncomfortable. This was very different than the dress-up parties in the Air Force and New Jersey. I scanned the women in the room and observed lots of wraparound skirts, Peter Pan-collared blouses, and Shetland sweaters. The men were without jackets and definitely no ties. The assessment was quick and the solution even quicker. Quick was the operative word. Ben took off his tie and jacket, and I removed my jacket, and rolled up the sleeves of my blouse. In about ten seconds (we could have become a magic act!), we reappeared as one of the casual couples and settled down to enjoy the people and the food. We had passed one of many hurdles in this new adventure. We reinvented ourselves and learned to dress down, not to dress up.

There would be many more cocktail parties. House parties in our area were more prevalent because we were not near larger cities that offered gourmet restaurants, theatre, or sports events. Philadelphia was sometimes a little too far to travel for a night out.

The first fundraiser we went to was an event for Mark Castile when he ran for governor. An important group of professionals and business people supported Mark Castile with donations and enthusiasm, and Ben and I decided we liked him. He was down-to-earth, likeable and had much experience as lieutenant governor. Halfway through the evening we found ourselves standing next to him. We were introduced and began to chitchat about some issues of the day. I had recently been informed by a new teacher friend about punishment in the school system. As a former teacher and also a parent, I was appalled at finding out that, in the state of Delaware, spanking a child in school was considered acceptable as a punishment for bad behavior. So I stepped out on a limb.

"Why would such punishment be OK in this day and age?" I inquired.

Ben chimed in, "Medically, I would classify this as child abuse. There would be no way to gauge the severity of a physical spanking or the emotional damage on a child."

"Well," Mr. Castile defensively answered, "we had serious problems of discipline with unruly kids in Delaware in the past, and it called for desperate measures. Parents were no help and we needed to have control. Then the law was passed enabling corporal punishment in the schools."

"With all due respect," I contended, my face turning red with emotion. "I, as a parent, retain the right to be the only person on the planet allowed to spank my child. The state has no right to interfere with personal parenting practices. I find the law deplorable and would challenge and certainly take to the highest court anyone who would dare strike my child!"

What I didn't know then was that, in 1975, a Supreme Court ruling held that schools could spank students against the wishes of their parents, subject to various criteria being met. In 1977, the same court held that paddling of school students was not, per se, unlawful. The constitutional law stipulation was that school corporal punishment be reasonable and not excessive. I think the soon-to-be governor was taken aback, and as several people were now approaching, the subject was rapidly dropped.

Ben and I were invited to the inauguration of the new governor, probably because of our donation. As we passed through the receiving line, I shook hands with Mark Castile and said, "Do you remember me, Governor?"

"Indeed I do, Bobbie," he said, calling me by name. "Maybe someday the law we discussed will be repealed." He winked and smiled.

That someday turned out to be too long into the future— Delaware did not ban spanking in the schools till 2003.

Chapter 19

While we were nicely settling into our more relaxed lifestyle, the practice of medicine was becoming more unsettled for Ben. After working in the new office several months, he called me at home, very perplexed.

"You know, Bobbie, I have come across the strangest thing," he said. "Almost all the elderly patients I am seeing each day are on the medication Dilantin. Dilantin is a medication prescribed for epilepsy. So that means one of several things: either everyone is having seizures or the elderly population is being sedated. I have been trying to get these patients off this medication, and it's really hard. They like being in la-la land. I tried talking to Dr. Morrow about this, but he told me that this is the way they do things down here. I can see I have my work cut out for me. Also, he came in yesterday to discuss with me my concern with annual physicals and testing; he did not want me to embark on any preventive medicine programs. He told me 'to treat only what I see.'"

I know Ben was very disturbed about this. Things were not going just as he had envisioned them. But his patients loved him, even the ones he weaned off Dilantin. He introduced a new way of health care to the elderly, one which could predict an outcome based on prevention. This is what forced him to overlook the negatives he was facing and made him press on.

Press on is what he did. There was a great deal of pressure from the local hospital to admit patients and keep the hospital beds filled. Obviously, occupied beds brought in more revenue. Ben's philosophy was to keep patients out of the hospital, so he was clashing with Dr. Morrow and hospital administrators on that issue. Also, the hospital labs were not responding like he thought they should. If a blood test was sent over to the hospital to process, it took forever to get results back. Ben had no patience for that. When an EKG needed to be over-read by the cardiologist on staff, it might take a week to be done. Ben liked to let his patients know their test results in a reasonable amount of time. He didn't like them to wait and worry. That was not taking place, and he was quite frustrated. Something had to give! And it did.

Medicine and health care had to give. The country was entering a new decade and there was bound to be change. Even though physicians stood high in the public esteem, people wanted something. In many measures of health care, the United States lagged behind other nations. There were inequalities in the access to health care, and costs were rising out of control. Medicine's old traditions were being challenged.

In the '60s, Medicare and Medicaid were signed into law. In the '70s, costs of these programs were escalating out of control. There was a big shift to the corporate way of delivering health care as healthcare costs became a great concern to citizens and government. Financing was largely fee for service, partly covered by private health insurance. But a person's state of health and chance of getting good medical care depended on who the person was, how much money the person had, and where the person lived.

Overall, there was too little attention paid to keeping people well. Changing social customs caused a rise in health problems, such as venereal disease, drug abuse, and HIV. This added to soaring health costs. New technology and scientific knowledge fueled the American philosophy "nothing was too expensive where one's health was concerned."

The doctor was caught right in the middle of the dilemma. Patients were upset if they didn't have the benefit of up-to-the-minute procedures. They wanted a diagnosis fast and a cure even faster. They wanted every problem they presented to be cured by a prescription for some pill. In many cases, however, it became clear that a cure was nearly always more expensive than prevention.

At this point in his career, Ben felt very confident and comfortable that his approach of preventing ill health was the right path to keep health costs down. The doctor he was working with had no interest in this and chose traditional medicine that focused only on the cure. Two different philosophies in the same office were just not working, so Ben made the difficult decision to go back to solo practice. When his contract was over, he rented an office in town and sent notices to the patients he was caring for. Much to Ben's surprise, almost all of his regular patients transferred their records to the new office.

I helped hire a nurse and receptionist and, once more, Dr. K. was going it alone.

As word got out that Ben also practiced occupational medicine, he was sought out by the few industries in southern Delaware. The Delaware State Police became an account as well as Purdue. In addition, International Latex, manufacturer of space suits for NASA, hired him as a medical consultant.

This was another very important contract, and he almost didn't get it. There was a doctor, who had been in the area a long time and had also applied for the position. When Ben was awarded the contract, he sensed there was a lot of animosity on the other doctor's part. I believe Ben was still deemed an outsider at this point and probably should not even have been considered for the opening. But he had great experience from the Air Force with several teams of astronauts and wound up serving this space suit program well.

The office was running smoothly until Ben's nurse became pregnant and gave notice. I heard that Dale, a nurse who worked in the hospital ER, wanted to work in a private doctor's office. I agreed to interview her. The interview was going quite well, and I proceeded to tell her what her duties would be. I included a request: that, since she would arrive before the doctor, could she start the coffee and put a cup of it on the doctor's desk before he began his day.

"Listen," she contended, "it's enough that I have to make coffee for my husband in the morning. I don't want to have to make it for the doctor. It's not in my job description."

"Well, I'm the doctor's wife, but when I enter the bathroom and see paper towels on the floor or the sink looking dirty, I clean up, and guess what? That's not in my job description either!"

Dale got the message and the job. Everything worked out well, as she worked alongside Dr. K. every day, once she set the cup of coffee on his desk each morning.

Chapter 20

Two decades had passed since Ben entered the world of medicine as a caregiver. As a physician dedicated to understanding his patient's physical and emotional needs, he was a winner. He was a doctor in the trenches, a first line of defense in the battle of keeping people alive and healthy. No easy task!

As a family physician, he had to know something about everything. When he didn't have the answers, he had to know when to refer his patients to a specialist who had them. His skills had to be constantly sharpened and updated, all the while maintaining that important relationship with his patients. He accomplished all this.

I think trust was the key word. His patients trusted him and he tried very hard never to let them down. He was a very conscientious, dedicated physician who never gave up. I feared he would burn out way too soon, but he seemed to keep a balance in his life. Family, friends, and personal activities made up that balance, and his sense of humor tied it all together.

I observed him with his patients and witnessed his compassion and concern. I watched him settle their fears and make them laugh. Ben was the measure by which I judged all other doctors. Of course, not all his patients felt as I did. There were those who were stubborn about health issues or ignorant about what they needed to do about good health. There were patients who were just cranky or too nonchalant about listening to advice. All of this made his job much more difficult.

There were patients, however, who stick in my mind as a tribute to his character as a caregiver. There were two young men, George and Charles, roommates, who checked in as new patients the week I was helping at the front desk. They were nervous and skittish, so I smiled and tried to put them at ease before they saw the doctor. After their visit, they needed a referral to a general surgeon, which I was able to make. I assured them that the surgeon was good, and they need not worry. I made them a follow-up visit, wrote out a referral slip, and sent them on their way, content and seemingly relieved.

They returned several days later appearing agitated; I led them back to the exam room. A few minutes later Ben came out to the front desk and told me to get the surgeon he had referred his patients to on the phone. He took the call in his own office. I could hear him shouting from his desk in the back of the office all the way to the front desk where I was, but could not make out what he was saying. When the two young men checked out with me, they seemed in good humor. I wondered what that had been all about.

As a rule, Ben and I never discussed patient cases, so I remained curious for months. George and Charles became regular patients along with several of their male friends. The staff and I had picked up on the fact that George and Charles might have been gay, which was confirmed when they felt comfortable enough to share it with us. It made absolutely no difference to any of us. I was still curious, however, as to what had happened on their second visit.

Because I worked in the office, I had access to patient information. When I asked Ben what all the shouting was about at the time of their visit, he was able to tell me in good conscience. I took my job very seriously and knew it was confidential.

Both men had been referred to the surgeon's office for anal surgical problems. After the surgeon treated the problems successfully, he proceeded to embark on a lecture telling the patients that their lifestyle was not right, and it would cause further health issues for them. He told them they needed counseling, perhaps through their church, and should realize their behavior was not normal. They needed to change their ways. He lectured them for ten minutes. They were mortified.

When they told Ben, he became enraged, prompting the call to the surgeon, saying, "How dare you lecture my patients. I sent them to you to correct a physical problem, not to self-righteously try and correct their lifestyle. That shows lack of respect, and you totally stepped out of bounds. Don't ever pull that on any of my patients again, or I will stop referrals to you!"

I applauded.

Peggy, a lovely, sweet, forty-year-old woman, was one of our cancer patients. She was a smoker, and lung cancer was picked up on a routine spirometer test and confirmed by an X-ray. She went through all the rigors of surgery and chemotherapy and returned to Ben for a regular follow-up. She had lost all her hair and her Medicaid insurance after her treatment. The day she came into the office she was in tears.

"I can't come here anymore, Dr. K." she announced. "I have no way to pay. They told me I have six months to live." Breaking down in Ben's office, she cried, "I only want to live long enough to attend my youngest son's high school graduation in two years."

"Peggy," Ben offered, "you are going to be at that graduation, but here is what I want you to do. You need to come into the office once a week. I want to monitor you, be aware of any problems that would set you back, be able to get to them early and get you to that graduation."

"But they cancelled my Medicaid, so I have no insurance. I can't pay you, Dr. K.," Peggy explained.

"There's no need to worry about that," he said, "because there are no charges. You will get to your son's graduation!"

For two years Peggy was a fixture in the office, and we all became very close to her and her family. She made it to the graduation with bells on, and it was a satisfying day for Dr. K. and all of the office, when she came in with her pictures of the important and happy event. We clapped and cheered and drank in the warmth of her smile that day. There were also a lot of tears, mostly on Ben's face.

The tears flowed again when, six months later, Peggy died. Ben was at the funeral giving comfort to her family. They included him in her eulogy and could not stop thanking him for helping her fulfill her most precious wish.

One of the contracts that Ben undertook was for the medical care of the Delaware State Police. The girls working in the office were always very happy when these patients came in, and they would all but swoon. Many times it was to have their blood drawn. They would enter in their starched, blue uniforms, looking macho and impressive. These men were almost always burly and well-built. They seemed stern and detached. So, it was amusing to hear them argue with the nurse about having to have their blood drawn. We soon found out why, when several of them passed out while enduring the needle and syringe used to take blood. They had tough exteriors but were soft and human at heart. When a trooper collapsed, it took two nurses to put him back into a sitting position. Dale, the RN, would coerce them into finally giving their blood samples without fear. Though the girls loved when the troopers came to the office, they loved it more when on occasion they were stopped for speeding while driving, and the trooper, recognizing them, would just warn them and, without a ticket, send them on their way.

There were other perks working for Dr. K. and his staff. Pharmaceutical companies would sponsor seminars and gourmet dinners, and we would go. Some of the reps would send small gifts at holiday time and occasionally fruit baskets and candy. The reps from these companies were grateful to the girls for getting them in to see the doctor. The reps would spend a few minutes briefing the doctor on new medications. The office was always responsive, since Ben wanted that info to keep current on any new medications.

Another group of patients who came into the office worked at a chicken raising and processing company located in lower Delaware. These patients were a challenge because there were a disproportionate number of them suffering from upper respiratory problems. These patients had to be followed closely per OSHA requirements. They were counseled to be aware of contact with chicken feathers, dander, dust, and feces, and to avoid inhaling any of these. The spirometer was a great aid in diagnosing COPD.

The area near Milford was farm country. Farmers also were showing up with a lot of upper respiratory symptoms. These became more prevalent at planting and harvesting times when the earth was in a state of being dug up. The dust was insidious. Ben instructed those patients involved to wear masks to filter out the dust and dirt.

There were all sorts of medical problems that were seen in this office that were never an issue in the New Jersey office and vice versa. For example, Ben saw more geriatric patients in Delaware, as that area had become a good retirement destination. In New Jersey, he saw more children, as younger couples moved into the suburbs.

In both locations, however, one couldn't escape the politics of medical practice. There was the American Medical Association, a respected group, who, in my opinion, did next to nothing for the average physician. There was the State Medical Society and the County Medical Society who worked harder for the physicians but also did not always respond to their needs. Ben became active in these local groups hoping to keep current in medical politics, trying to change what he was not happy with, but politics on a very local level was tuned in to the good ol' boys mentality and was sometimes unjust. Because of the small area of practice, referrals generally were limited to just a few doctors, and if a physician referred too far out of that circle, he became politically incorrect. Small, rural, medical communities claimed the advantage of making up their own unspoken rules.

Ben had an elderly, male patient of long standing, who was having severe back problems and needed a consult to determine if surgery might be warranted. Ben referred him to a new doctor of an orthopedic group. Our office received a report stating that no surgery would be done.

"I will call the orthopedist and find out how our patient made out," Dr. K. told us.

When he talked to the orthopedist, he was given this news: "I'll be seeing the patient from now on, and I can handle all his medical needs, so that's why you had no further report."

"Are you kidding?" Ben questioned. "I sent the patient for an opinion and consult. Why would you treat his general health?"

There was some flip answer returned to Ben and the conversation ended abruptly. The next call was to Dr. Flynn, who owned the group. Ben had referred to him a lot and had always been satisfied. Ben voiced his concern as to why his group would be stealing a patient of his.

After hearing of the problem, Dr. Flynn agreed with Ben and advised him, "This sometimes happens, but I will look into it."

Of course, no follow-up call was ever received, but we heard by the grapevine that Dr. Flynn came down hard on the orthopedist. It was almost six months later that we heard that this doctor left the group and started a practice in a neighboring town, my guess being that the doctor brought with him many patients acquired from other practices.

We had now entered the era of health care in the '80s. Issues were changing rapidly. The first test-tube baby clinic opened in the United States. The surgeon general reported the first signs of an epidemic of smoking-related diseases among women. Restriction of federal financing of abortions under Medicaid was ruled unconstitutional, and genetically engineered interferon (a disease-fighting protein) was produced. HIV was becoming a severe, fearful health problem to the point that people did not even want to kiss each other on the cheek. In the meantime the delivery of health care was becoming more corporatized in an effort to curb costs, and a rationing of high tech care and preventive primary care was starting to happen.

Where was medicine and health care heading? I guess the "good ol' days" were gone forever!

Chapter 21

In the years since Ben proudly received his medical degree, amazing advances had come about in the field of medicine. Perhaps the good ol' days were not that good after all, because in the '60s, '70s, and '80s life-altering events came about that totally changed the medical world. By the year 1983, more than a dozen "firsts" had made news.

1962 - First oral polio vaccine (as an alternative to the injected vaccine)
1964 - First vaccine for measles
1967 - First vaccine for mumps
1967 - First human heart transplant by South African heart surgeon Dr. Christian Barnard
1970 - First vaccine for rubella
1974 - First vaccine for chicken pox
1977 - First vaccine for pneumonia
1978 - First test-tube baby in the UK
1980 - WHO (World Health Organization) announces smallpox is eradicated
1981 - First vaccine for hepatitis B
1982 - Dr. William De Vries implants the Jarvik-7 artificial heart into patient Barney Clark who lives 112 days
1983 - HIV, the virus that causes AIDS, is identified.

It was an exciting time for physicians. They were being given important armaments to combat disease and sickness; however, the practice of medicine with all its negative aspects and outside interference was very frustrating. Those physicians true to their profession seemed to ignore the negatives and plodded on, doing what they did best, striving to make people's lives better.

Despite the changes taking place in the profession, medical school applications rose to an all-time high in the late 1980s, and schools then, as now, received three to five times more applicants than they had positions for. It appeared that medicine was among the higher paying and most prestigious professions in the country. But, if someone is only interested in the money, they should look for other fields. There are many other jobs with a higher entry level salary and easier credentialing.

"So, Ben," I asked softly, one evening when we had kissed David goodnight and were sitting down to a second cup of coffee, in front of our brightly burning fireplace. "Why did you really want to become a doctor?"

He looked at me thoughtfully. "I don't know" was his immediate response. "I just always wanted to look after people, I guess. When I was in college and had to pick a direction, it was a no-brainer for me. I made a list of pros and cons of going into medicine, and even after my cons list was much longer than my pros list, I didn't change my mind. Why do you ask? Do you think I made a mistake? Maybe you would have been happier marrying someone in a different line of work."

"No, no, no, that's not what I was leading to," I quickly replied. "But I would be interested in what your list had on it."

"I believe it was a lopsided list. For instance on the pro side I had the desire to help people and the ability to do something important with my life, to be part of an interesting and challenging profession, and to be able to support my family without worry. Now, on the con side I listed long study time, endless learning, long hours, lack of sleep, great responsibility, on-call hours, stress, and important decisions. Plus, I have to face that if I made one mistake, it could cost a life. If I had been aware of the malpractice situation, I would have listed that as a definite fear. Scary, isn't it?"

"Well, I think you made the right choice," I assured him. "In fact, I'm sure of it!"

We talked long after our coffee cups were empty, and the fire had gone out. We sat with Ben's arms encircling me and patted ourselves on the back for our solid and happy marriage and for the terrific kids we had. I threw praises at Ben for being such a successful physician in every aspect as well as a great husband and father, and he threw praise back with the most complimentary words. We stared at the pictures on the mantel: Scott, who was now a senior in college; Michael, a junior in college; and David, who was in sixth grade. They were exceptionally nice children. We were feeling very lucky!

Life was good in our little rural part of the country, but not in the rest of the world. A huge medical problem that was emerging was the spreading of AIDS worldwide. Each country was grappling with how to cope with the spreading of this disease, especially in regard to international travel. Ben had already seen cases of HIV in patients who had vacationed in foreign places. He sent them to Philadelphia to hospitals that were more equipped to fight this virus. The problem was growing in outrageous numbers and patients were turning to their physicians for answers to the problem. Everyone seemed to be in a panic mode!

The timing for the invitation Ben received for a high-level meeting, in all places, Paris, France, was perfect. It was entitled AIDS and the WORKPLACE, Medical Aspects. It was under the high patronage of Mr. Jacques Delors, President of the Commission of the European Communities, in collaboration with the World Health Organization. We suspected that due to Ben's background in occupational medicine, he had been included to participate in the solving of this frightening health issue. Ben decided to attend and take me with him as his acting secretary. The meeting agenda sounded interesting and important, and with Ben feeling very honored, we were soon off to Paris in the springtime.

April in Paris started for us when we arrived at Charles De Gaulle airport and hailed a taxi to our newly renovated hotel on the right bank of the River Seine. After freshening up, we ventured out, French dictionary in hand, to get a feel for the city before it became dark.

We were so happy we had decided to extend this trip into a vacation following a work week. We had made plans with our friends Pat and Charlie to meet us in Paris after the conference, spend three days sightseeing Paris, and then take the infamous Venice Simplon-Orient-Express to Venice, Italy, and spend another five days touring Venice and Rome. I had always wanted to ride on the Orient-Express. It was definitely on my bucket list. I had read all the Agatha Christie novels, with my favorite being *Murder on the Orient Express*. The most beloved character of that book is Poirot, the detective and hero of many of her books. Just the idea of what we would be doing was thrilling to me. I had seen the movie *Murder on the Orient-Express* three times and I was totally geared up to be on that train!

We cut our stroll short, stopped at a café for a quick supper, and returned to our hotel before our bodies could realize the different time zone. The time change took hold, as we were awake, perky, and anxious to get to the conference. We dressed and ate in a hurry and soon found ourselves in front of an elaborate, gold-adorned building with luxurious black wrought iron trim.

"This building is magnificent," Ben marveled.

"It's just gorgeous!" I agreed.

We walked up the long flight of stairs to the top and the huge intricately carved wooden doors. When we went inside, we were in awe. The rotunda we found ourselves in was more regal than any palace we had ever seen in pictures or in real life. We entered the conference hall and were stunned. It was a huge room that resembled a room at the United Nations building, with podiums and seats arranged in a semi-circle. Earphones stood at attention at each place. We were quickly ushered to our seats as the opening welcome speech was getting underway in French. Representatives from all around the world, including us, scurried to adjust the earphones. The meeting had officially begun.

During the next three days, intense presentations and discussions were held with the delegates voting on a myriad of subjects, such as the following:

> Worldwide distribution of HIV/AIDS
> Trends and projections in HIV/AIDS
> Priorities in the early 1990s
> Advisory bodies
> Women, children, and AIDS
> Avoidance of discrimination in relation to HIV-infected
>   people and people with AIDS
> Collaboration with nongovernmental organizations
> World AIDS Day
> National program monitoring
> Intervention development and support
> Clinical research and drug development
> Vaccine development
> Diagnostics
> Epidemiological support and research
> Surveillance forecasting and impact assessment
> Collaboration within the United Nations system

The body of delegates resolved all the issues, but the biggest issue, international travel with AIDS, was not globally concluded. Each country was in the process of setting its own standards and laws, and at that time this seemed to be the only acceptable answer of AIDS crossing borders. In 1987, responding to fears that HIV-infected immigrants could threaten public health as well as economic stability, the Department of Health and Human Services added AIDS to the list of diseases that could exclude a traveler from getting a visa to enter the United States. Later that year, Congress enacted legislation mandating HIV screening for all visa applicants over the age of fourteen. As imagined, there was a great deal of protest, and all international meetings were scheduled outside of the United States. In 2008 Congress took action removing regulatory language about travel and immigration restrictions, and in 2009, the travel ban was lifted.

After three ten-hour days, our mission at the conference was accomplished, and we soon received a call that our friends had arrived. We continued our stay in Paris with them and looked forward to our reservation on the infamous Orient-Express train to Venice, Italy.

The next three days were a blur of sightseeing, shopping, wine drinking, and eating the richest food and most decadent desserts on the planet. It was perfect! When we were sure we couldn't possibly eat another soufflé, crêpe suzette, crème brûlée, cream puff, or truffle, it was time to waddle to the station to meet our overnight home on the Orient-Express. When we arrived, we were all overwhelmed by the old, restored, turn-of-the-century train station and the rehabilitated, huge, shiny, black locomotive standing by to welcome us aboard. When the starched, white uniformed porter came over to greet us and take our luggage, I knew we were off on the trip of a lifetime. A whistle softly blew, and steam seemed to come from nowhere beckoning us to step up and get on.

"All aboard!" shouted the conductor.

"With pleasure," we all replied in unison.

A red carpet was then rolled out for the passengers, and we walked to the train feeling very special. In my wildest dreams I could not have imagined the luxury my eyes gazed upon after boarding the magnificent coach car. We were on the world's most celebrated train, and it was fit for a king. Some of the corridors were lined with mahogany wall panels with etched marquetry, giving them a 3-D effect, and others had glass panels designed by Lalique, the French glass designer. A 1920s' art deco design prevailed. Old carriage lamps, with off-white, pleated silk shades were on the walls, along with tulip-shaped Lalique opaque glass lamps. Cut red velvet defined the curtains, and much of the upholstery in each compartment was made of heavy, floral brocade.

"This is stunning," I whispered.

The compartments were quite small, but lavish. They appeared just as I had seen them recreated in countless movies. It was a bit of a hassle to store our luggage in the small space, but we successfully did and managed to dress for dinner on time; the evening attire was formal. Ben looked grand in his tuxedo, and I felt elegant in my black, sequined, floor-length dress. Our friends met us in the club car for cocktails, followed by a white glove, elaborate five-course dinner in the dining car. After dinner, according to our plan, we went to the club car where the guys smoked cigars and sipped brandy. My friend and I pulled out long, tapered cigarette holders we had purchased and inserted our French cigarettes.

"Look at us," I declared.

With a lot of attitude we sat and smoked and sipped our brandy, looking quite sophisticated and chic. It was a moment in time that was priceless, and we did not want to break the mood, so we did not retire until two in the morning. We were quickly lulled to sleep by the soft click-clack of the train's wheels on the tracks, and the promise of a great tomorrow.

The next day after a sumptuous breakfast, we settled back in our coach seats to watch the slideshow of panoramic scenery from the windows. The snow-encrusted Alps in their majestic glory made an unusual backdrop for the small towns and villages; antique-looking houses whizzed by. The time passed so quickly, and before we had fully absorbed the splendor of what we were viewing, we were approaching our destination of Venice, Italy.

What a contrast! After disembarking from the Orient-Express and walking out of the station, we were stunned. We had left miles of glorious snow-covered mountains and valleys of green hills and now were surrounded by water as far as the eye could see. There was water everywhere! Gondolas raced toward us and the other newly disembarked train passengers. These were the water taxis, which we hailed exactly as we would have in the middle of New York City.

After a lively boat ride to our hotel, we settled in for a two-day adventure. We were on the go for ten hours each day and managed to see everything wonderful about Venice. We walked where we could through the little villages. Most of our time though, was spent on beautifully decorated gondolas, some with singing oarsmen. We enjoyed some great meals and wine while we cruised around the city, delighting in the magnificent, ancient architecture.

It ended all too soon. It was back on a train for us, not nearly as grand as the one we had just been on, but it was called a bullet train for a reason. It was incredibly fast and we arrived in Rome in record time.

Rome was all that I had read about and even more. We had two days to drink in all the wonders this city had to offer. It surprised us with its amazing contrast of modern buildings and age-worn, historic sites like the Pantheon, the Colosseum, the Roman Forum, St. Peter's Basilica, and an extraordinary group of buildings that belong to the Vatican. We threw coins into the Trevi Fountain and made lots of wishes. We also managed to enjoy many Italian delicacies, too many bowls of pasta, great Italian wine, and richer than rich desserts.

"I can't believe this incredible vacation is ending," I cried, as we boarded our plane to return home to reality.

Although I missed the children, I could have easily stayed for at least another month, or two.

Chapter 22

Reality seemed a bit harsh when we returned. My mom was diagnosed with cancer, and we moved her to our home, with my Dad, to live out her last six months. It was really tough, but I would like to think that our family added much warmth, humor, and love to her last days. Ben became so frustrated. He knew he was helpless to cure her, so he tried to make her more comfortable. He brought home some liquid pain medication, but being stubborn, she refused to take it. She maintained that she wanted to be clearheaded to see and talk with the family. I guess I couldn't blame her.

"I'm able to help so many people, but I can't do a thing for my own mother-in-law," Ben lamented, day after day in great despair.

I still have to laugh when I think of the time I was called upon to give her a suppository to help control her nausea from the chemotherapy. I told her to bend over the tub and lift her nightgown. It was obvious she was mortified and tears welled up in her eyes.

"Listen, Mom," I softly said, "It's OK. I'm just getting even for all those times you had to give me suppositories when I was a little girl."

The whole mood was broken. She had a twinkle in her eye while she laughed all the way back to her bed. It was visualizing that twinkle that really got me through the day of my best friend's funeral.

Ben's practice began to be even busier than before we had left for vacation. The idea of the value of preventive medicine began to arouse interest, and more and more new patients were making appointments for complete physical examinations. The patients were being counseled on health issues based on what some of their testing revealed. Ben tried to urge his patients not to ask for antibiotics so frequently. He felt they were being overused and might even be ineffective someday. He preached this, but it didn't seem to do any good. Everyone still wanted antibiotics.

More complicated screening blood tests were being done,

which gave the doctor and patient, a heads-up approach to many ailments. More and more patients were getting referred to the hospital nutritionist to learn to eat right for good health. The new programs were very successful and popular with the patients. The downside was that Ben was now working harder and harder, and I got to see him less and less.

"So, I never get to see you much these days," I implied one evening. "Maybe we should make a date night soon."

"I guess you just can't have everything," he replied. "I feel like I do a lot of self-sacrificing that no money can really compensate for, but so be it. Even with taking our vacations now and then, I guess I am just plain tired, extremely tired. Thank you for sacrificing with me. It's why I love you so much."

I got the tired part. Our vacation certainly refreshed us temporarily, but after a week back in the office, it was like we never had been away. It was getting very difficult to comply with all the rules and regulations put on physicians' medical practices. Personally, I was getting weary of all the attacks on the profession and the constant barrage of media blasting and blaming doctors for the high cost of health care. Doctors actually made up ten percent of total healthcare costs. The media were really attacking the wrong amounts, not where the real costs were.

I even had a friend say to me, "I see you have a new car. I guess the office fees will now increase."

Did they really think that was how the decision to raise fees was implemented? I guess they never realized that fees go up due to the cost of doing business. A medical practice is, in truth, very much like any business. If the cost of the janitor went up, if paper prices went up, if the cost of other medical supplies increased, if the rent changed, if insurance went up, if the employees needed a raise, then fees increased. At the same time, payments from various private and government insurance companies stayed the same or in some cases went down.

Since preserving life is the most important work anyone can do, the work of physicians is the most important of human endeavors. With that in mind, doctors who provided health care were actually undercompensated. People seemed to have no problem with CEOs, athletes, musicians, and actors making millions of dollars, but physicians were expected to be self-denying. People gladly paid one hundred dollars for a sporting event but went into a rage if they had to pay a thirty-dollar co-pay on their insurance. Private practice was a catch-22 situation for doctors. Also, I could never understand why some people were so bent out of shape about doctors' salaries. They certainly did not make more, for example, than corporate heads, bankers, lawyers, or politicians.

My question back to my friend was, "Considering the importance of the profession in keeping people alive and well, why do you care if physicians make a decent living?"

I'm still waiting for the answer.

It was in those times that I started to get worried about our future. Almost every day we were getting directives from different agencies supposedly concerned with cost cutting and ethics in medicine. For example, some directives were made up by congressmen, who were constantly showered with favors, gifts, and perks, but who thought it a crime if a doctor accepted lunch from a drug company representative.

The Medicare announcement I received the day of our return was the epitome of bureaucratic nonsense.

"Can you believe this?" I bellowed throughout the entire office. "We have been helping Medicare patients for years by not billing them the difference between their insurance and actual costs, and now this notice says we must bill and collect that difference from the patient. The doctor has no free will to help his patients financially. This is insane. If not complied with, the doctor will receive sanctions."

I was in a frenzy, but after a while, I realized I could do nothing but notify the patients and listen to their grumbling.

I had instituted a policy that I found very effective. Sometimes patients just could not pay their bill. Dr. K. still wanted them to come in for their health problems, so we had a policy that if you owed on a bill, you could pay it off with no interest. We would accept as little as one dollar a week, as long as an effort was made to pay the debt. There were times we accepted chickens or garden-grown vegetables as payment from some of the local farmers. This worked so beautifully because it enabled those patients who were having hard times to keep their dignity and not be afraid to come back to see the doctor. However, it did at times cause a cash crunch for our office, which was a great concern. There were also those who simply ignored paying, and they had to be dropped from the practice.

Ben gave so much of his time in those years. We did not have a policy in the office of time constraints. If a patient was having a complicated problem, then Ben would take the extra minutes to absorb his issue and help him find a solution. The patients who had to wait in the waiting room a few more minutes seemed willing to do so, because they knew if ever they needed some extra time, they would get it. Ben rarely spent less than twenty minutes with each patient, which was considered a regular office visit. He also returned phone calls received during the day after five o'clock; everyone who called that day received a call back.

The real problem was that medicine was evolving to such a level of technology it was becoming unaffordable. The simple act of the patient being given time to talk and the doctor to listen was slowly disappearing. The doctor-patient relationship was being affected in a most negative way. Talking to the patient was a very cost-effective tool, and it was sad that medicine was sacrificing it because insurance companies would not pay.

Some of the patients really took advantage of our office and the doctor. They were few in number, but discouraging and annoying. When an insurance company would not pay for a procedure, and we had to bill the patient, a struggle would ensue with these patients. We had a mother and her teenage son as patients, and the son had a physical examination. The insurance company paid for all but one test, and after we billed for it, the mother came storming into the office.

"I am not paying for this test," she belligerently declared. "He never had this test."

The patient's chart was pulled, and in the notes, it showed the test had been done and results recorded by the nurse. Even after we showed her the chart (which in today's world we would not be permitted to do), she stormed out of the office with a promise not to pay.

Each month we billed the mother, and after nine months of not receiving payment, I made the decision to take the matter to small claims court. It was a nerve-racking experience for me. There was an appearance before a judge, who questioned the mother and myself and then looked over and reviewed the patient chart. He determined that the test had been done, with the results plainly stated in the chart. The mother was ordered to pay the bill along with court costs, which she ultimately did. I was not happy about the entire situation, but what were we to do?

On Dr. K.'s desk there was a little framed saying in quotations: "A living is based on what you get. A life is based on what you give." I found myself questioning the part about "what you give."

But "give" is what Ben did. There were so many occasions he was called upon for his medical help while not in the office. Medical emergencies happened to family and friends all the time. When asked, Ben never failed to respond. Most often the issues were minor or, at times, advice was needed. He would always step up, respond, and take care of the needs of those who called on him. I was so proud of his generosity.

Some of those incidents of medical care were pretty funny. I recall one when we were leaving for vacation, and we were passing through Philadelphia Airport. As we were checking our luggage, someone called out to Ben. It was the deputy director of the airport, also a patient of his.

"Dr.K., boy am I happy to see you. I was about to call you. I have a big problem. My physical exam for my FAA license is overdue, and I need to see you right away."

"Well, it's a bigger problem than you think," Ben told him. "I am leaving within the hour on vacation and will not be back for two weeks."

"Oh no, what will I do?"

Ben thought for a moment and asked him if he knew of an airline reception room nearby. He did and the two of them disappeared inside where Ben performed a physical examination on the man, thereby saving his license. That was one man happy with his doctor.

Another one of many incidents happened while we were with our friends on a bus touring Yellowstone Park. Our friend Charlie had been having some difficulty with his back and was in severe pain. Luckily, Ben always carried medication with him, so he was able to give a dose to Charlie, but the pain was still persistent.

"You need some of the analgesic cream I have rubbed on your back," Ben advised him.

"We won't be off this bus for another two hours," said Charlie.

"OK, then follow me," Ben directed.

He took him to the bathroom at the rear of the bus, had him take off his shirt, and proceeded to rub his back with the cream. All the while Charlie was calling out, "Oh, that feels so good. Keep it up, a little bit more to the right."

When they emerged, they had to endure lots of stares and giggles for the next two hours. Even I giggled.

Of course, there were several episodes of Ben using the Heimlich maneuver in restaurants. Another incident involved a young man having severe stomach pains in an upscale German restaurant. Ben had him lay flat on the floor so he could examine his stomach to rule out appendicitis or anything else severe in nature. So, with customers almost stepping on the patient, Ben did his exam and determined that a trip to the men's room was all the patient needed. Physicians were constantly on call to rise to the occasion when called upon.

Not all those who had to rise to the call were physicians, however. There were those of us who were married to the person who was married to his profession. I, for one, realize what an important part I played by allowing Ben to have someone run interference for him. Having me in the office gave him a certain sense of security in knowing mistakes were at a minimum or nonexistent. He had no worries about his staff or any interface with patients. I kept the entire office running smoothly and enjoyed doing it.

I didn't enjoy, however, having to be the one sleeping next to the phone all the time and taking those middle-of-the-night emergency telephone calls. I was the one able to wake up quickly and still be coherent enough to talk to the hospital, while Ben woke up and took a minute or two to focus on the call. We worked as a team.

I know I was not the only one in this world who had to go to parties and events alone because her partner had to work. Ben showing up late for dinner engagements was routine. I always hoped the patients appreciated his time with them when it could have been spent with me. I realized my children were not the only ones who had a dad who missed most of their games or events. But realizing this didn't make it any better; however, that's just the way it was.

Chapter 23

Life in rural America was different, but it mostly lacked vitality. In the eight years we lived in Delaware, we experienced pig roasts, firehouse weddings, small town gossip, shopping on a limited scale, no theatre, and few really good restaurants. We enjoyed group picnics, horse and car races, house auctions of antiques, and the Delaware beaches. We also delighted in our special friends and lots of nice people. In general, our life seemed good, despite having to adjust to quiet living and Ben, once again, being on call most of the time. There was one thing that bothered us. Every time we went into Philadelphia for a change of scenery, we both longed to stay. There was a certain beat to the city that we missed very much. When we visited friends, we were constantly challenged by them to give reasons why we could not, or would not, move to Philadelphia.

On one of our cruises we met a lovely couple, a bit younger than us, from Philadelphia. We spent most of the two weeks of vacation with Larry and his beautiful wife Barbara; we all quickly became good friends and continued to see them after we returned home. Barbara and I became close, as we are to this day. Our son David was the same age as their two boys, so we visited back and forth quite often. It was on one of these visits that our friends urged Ben to leave his private practice in Delaware and come to Philadelphia to practice. Larry had contacts in the city and felt he could help Ben. He talked about rehabilitation medicine and Ben opening a physical therapy office. In that type of medicine, there would be no "on call." The offer certainly was very enticing, but the idea of moving again seemed out of the question. The upside was that Ben had a wonderful practice. He loved his patients and the feeling was mutual. The downside was that he was always working or on call, and after twenty-five years, it might be nice to have a practice where there was no watch on nights or weekends. We couldn't even imagine what that would be like. And then we started imagining.

It was 1986, and the older boys were in law school while the youngest was in high school. We could certainly consider a move again if it would give us more freedom and still enable Ben to do what he loved so much — practice his medicine. Being back in Philadelphia was a huge temptation, and we began to be ensnared by the thought of spending the last years of his career in the place where he started out.

"Do you think I should give up my medical practice here and all I have accomplished with my patients?" he kept asking me.

I had no answer for him. In all the years on this planet, I had discovered I could be happy anywhere. Happiness, after all, is a state of mind.

"But, here we go again. You've made some nice friends here. How could I ask you to start all over?" he asked.

Sometimes I hated it when my answers were quotes from something I had read.

"Listen," I retorted. "Strangers are simply friends we haven't met."

It sounded so simple but it was exactly how I wanted it to sound. I needed him to make a solo decision and follow his own heart. I was along for the journey.

After many back and forth telephone conversations with our friend, Ben decided to take the leap. Now the fun began.

An offer was made to Ben to open a medical practice and physical therapy department with someone we were introduced to by our friend. Ben was not going to practice family medicine but would concentrate on occupational and rehabilitation medicine. After many discussions, terms were met and contracts were signed. Ben's partner was an entrepreneur by the name of Steven Epstein or "Eppy," as everyone called him. The partners opened a brand new center with up-to-date equipment and hired a physical therapist and several aides. A receptionist and computer person rounded out the staff. I agreed to be available to set things up and come in occasionally when needed. The center also employed a physiatrist and could x-ray on the premises. It was a well-equipped center, and Ben was excited to be involved.

As it turned out, Eppy was quite a classic. We loved him from the start. He was straight out of a Damon Runyon novel and could easily have been cast as one of the personalities in Runyon's *Guys and Dolls*.

One day, while I was sitting at my desk down the hall from Eppy's office, a group of handsome, well-dressed, middle-aged, black gentlemen walked past me, bent on going to Eppy's room. I asked them to identify themselves, but they ignored me and went striding toward his office. I caught up with them as they entered the office and was about to voice my displeasure when Eppy said, "Bobbie, I would like to introduce you to the Stylistics."

I think my mouth dropped open. I was starstruck. They were the most popular vocal group of the '70s and I had all their records. At that point, I opted not to voice my annoyance at them for ignoring me, and wisely so, as I walked away with their autographs and a fond memory.

Since Ben and I were pretty conservative people, Eppy brought a fresh breath into our lives. It was not unusual to see entertainers stopping into the office and mingling with or greeting the patients. We wound up treating some of them medically as well.

The best part of it all, we had our nights and weekends free. We were able to take out subscriptions to attend every performance at the Walnut Street Theatre and went to the Academy of Music on a weekly schedule. Saturday nights became delectable delights as we tried to visit every good restaurant in town, all the time feeling very grateful that we had made the right decision to return to the energetic and charming City of Brotherly Love.

About the same time we opened the new office, we had put our wonderful house in Delaware on the market, and I sold it in two days by myself. Moving day was very sad. When the movers left and the house was empty, my chest was heavy. David and I were handling it, though, with little drama, until we packed the last of our things into the car and drove down our long brick driveway. We were halfway down the road when the song "Yellow Brick Road" came on the radio. David turned it up and Elton John was blasting the words that seemed to have been written just for us—for this time—especially these verses:

> *"So good-bye yellow brick road*
> *Where the dogs of society howl*
> *You can't plant me in your penthouse*
> *I'm going back to my plough*
> *Back to the howling old owl in the woods*
> *Hunting the horny back toad*
> *Oh, I've finally decided my future lies*
> *Beyond the yellow brick road."*

It's funny what power songs have on our emotions. We both started to bawl and continued to cry for several miles, as we drove into the future, way beyond our own brick road.

In short order, we found a new, three-story, three-bedroom townhouse outside of the city. It had lots of stairs and lots of city style. There was really no yard space but a great deal of space inside with two fireplaces, white walls, and white carpet and tile. There was a wooden spiral staircase that climbed from the master bedroom to the overhang loft above, looking like something from *House Beautiful* magazine. It was elegant and really the change we needed.

David was enrolled in a small private high school and seemed to adjust quite well. Before long there were kids hanging out at our house. I begged them to take off their shoes as they came in, with hopes of preserving all that white carpet. They grudgingly complied. We saw Larry and Barbara often, and I made some lovely friends in the neighborhood. Ben and I began to have a social life, which included his partner Eppy.

"Do you guys gamble?" he asked Ben one day at the office. "I play poker and bet a lot at Caesars in Atlantic City, so I get complimentary rooms and food whenever I go. How about both of you joining me this weekend?"

"We'd love to, thanks," Ben replied. "But you need to know, that only my wife gambles; she plays the slots. Her big deal is to play the quarter machines. To me, money comes too hard to play it away, so I'll be happy to just watch you at the poker table."

We entered a whole new world the weekend we went to Caesars with Eppy. We watched people, well into the early morning, play poker with piles of chips worth thousands of dollars. We ate nonstop with Eppy and his entourage of friends at all the high-end restaurants in the casino. One night, at the Japanese restaurant in the casino, there were nine of us, and no one could decide what to eat, so Eppy told the waiters to bring one of everything on the menu. It was truly a banquet that might have been ordered by Caesar himself.

There were many fun times with Eppy. He was a laugh a minute in the office. Although he was only nine years younger than I was, he called me Mom and came to me for advice on most of his personal issues. When he was in the office, it was like a whirlwind passing through. I will always think of him fondly as the most unforgettable character I have ever had the pleasure of knowing.

Eppy mostly ran the office and I was the backup. We were getting patients from all over the city, and the office was running smoothly. The problem was space. We were running out of it. When the Exxon gas station across the street went up for sale, we made an offer and it was accepted. Our son Michael, an attorney, handled all the legal work. We had an architect draw up plans, and Exxon began to have all the gas tanks dug up and the property cleaned up per the Environmental Protection Agency regulations. Once that was done, we began to rehab the building and add more footage.

The new office was really shaping up and was nearly complete when the EPA came to do an inspection. We passed on every issue except a very important one. In the back of the building, we were told, there were oil deposits that had to be cleaned up. According to our understanding, Exxon needed to clean all residual from the gas station. They refused, saying they would only be responsible for the gas tanks, not anything else. They claimed the oil came from the draining of cars that was done inside. Therefore, not being on the outside of the property, even though that's where it emptied out to, it was not their problem. We argued with them to no avail; they had a staff of lawyers who gave us a bad time. So, wanting to move forward, we borrowed and paid $30,000 to clean up the oil per EPA requirements. Everything else was on schedule, and when the office was completed, it looked great. After all the equipment and furniture was moved over, we had an office opening for the neighborhood and other invited guests. There was a party atmosphere that Saturday, but bright and early on Monday morning, it was back to taking care of patients and the rigors of their physical therapy.

We knew we had a fight on our hands trying to make Exxon step up to their obligations. We felt like real underdogs.

"What should I do?" our son Michael asked. "It was really Exxon's duty to clean up that oil. Should I pursue the matter and try to make them pay?"

"How in the world can you make them pay? They're a big company with a stable of attorneys who will go to court and drag this out because they know we'll bend. It's not very promising," we told him.

"Well, I have an idea. I'll give them a call, and let's see what happens," he declared. Michael called the main number for the Exxon attorneys and put the phone on loud speaker so we could hear. He reached the attorney he had been dealing with and again reiterated our demand to be reimbursed for the oil cleanup. This lawyer all but laughed in his face and was very clear that they would not pay and told him to sue them if we must. He implied it was a joke to think that the partners had a chance with a big company like Exxon.

It was then the party turned ugly. Michael, in his quiet but determined way, spoke softly into the phone. "Sir, at this time I need to remind you what the reality of this situation is. Should all parties choose to settle this in the courts of Philadelphia, you need to get a clear picture of what will be taking place. The case will be heard in this city, with the jurors being chosen from citizens who live here. So, here you have a neighborhood doctor, who people know and respect, going up against a big corporation like Exxon, whose ship, the *Exxon Valdez*, is currently responsible for dumping gallons of crude oil in Prince William Sound, Alaska. Now, who do you think the jury will be siding with, the small guy, or the big, environmentally destructive company?"

There was dead silence on the other end of the phone.

The Exxon attorney snapped his answer. "I'll send the check for the full amount of $30,000 tomorrow with a release form for the partners to sign and return."

We heard a loud hang up click. Michael didn't even have a chance to say thank you.

Chapter 24

While Ben was finding satisfaction in his new clinic, the rest of the healthcare world seemed like it was in a state of dissatisfaction. Corporatized health care, which began in the '50s, was now a fact of life in the '80s. Corporate ownership of practices, clinics, and hospitals was a new reality. This became popular as a defense against out-of-control healthcare costs. Of course, in order to accomplish reduction of costs, some medical services had to be cut. Suddenly, the length of hospital stays was reduced and ancillary services were all but eliminated. At the same time, there seemed to be a battle for resources between preventive primary care and high-tech care, with no one winning. Hospitals needed updated facilities and were losing many patients to new facilities such as birthing centers, surgical centers, urgent care centers, physical therapy clinics, and hospices.

"You know, I really feel I have made a wise choice, given what's besieging private doctors' practices these days, but I do miss the kind of challenges I had in family medicine," Ben announced one day.

At this time, he became very interested in pain management and started to work toward becoming credentialed in that field. There was also a lot of hype about drug abuse in the late 1980s. Stories about cocaine and crack were dominant in the news with an emphasis on crack-babies being born in the big cities. There was a new healthcare panic taking place, and as drug use began to skyrocket, the costs to the healthcare system were overwhelming. The rules were also changing.

Dr. K. was a designated Department of Transportation physician, and drivers of commercial vehicles were required to have a complete physical examination before their license could be renewed.

One day, Dr. K. had an announcement: "All drivers now have to have a urine drug test, so several of you will take a course with me to learn how to do a chain of custody urinalysis."

That included me, and I actually became the main, test giver and certified Medical Review Officer. The chain of custody meant the urine sample had to be constantly in my sight till tested, and the results had to be recorded in a particular way so those results would be one hundred percent accurate. We were taught all the tricks a patient might use to try to get a good result on a test. They included bringing a friend's urine sample in a container (kept in a purse or pocket) and then switching it, or diluting the sample with water. So I had to strip-search every single patient before he or she went into the restroom and hold any purses. The water faucet had to be taped closed and dye put in the toilet bowl to avoid using any water. This was something I never thought I would be doing in my lifetime.

We had also entered the computer world in the office. Six IBM computers were networked so everyone had access to all the computers, except the one in billing. Most of the nurses and aides working in the office had no clue when it came to computers. I insisted that everyone learn and become proficient. I received nothing but resistance and complaining, until one day, annoyed, I spoke up.

"Listen up, girls. You need to pay attention to what I am telling you. Computers are in and if you are unable to use one, you will be out. Think of this: Dr. K. will not be practicing here forever. You might be forced to look for another job. Perhaps it will be in another office or hospital. The competition will be tough, and you need to be able to compete with everyone who is computer savvy. You need to be ahead of everyone, so let's get to it."

At the same time, I became privileged to observe the caring that was taking place in our physical therapy clinic. The doctor, therapists, and aides were all so gentle and encouraging. Patients came in with many physical setbacks. They came with canes, walkers, wheelchairs, and crutches. It was satisfying to see them walk out, after the proper length of treatment, and return to their former selves.

I think Dr. K. was most happy with patient outcomes because almost all of the maladies he was treating were not chronic, and he could always see the results of his efforts. The patients were happy because of everyone's attitude in the clinic. The dedication of the staff was very evident.

"You know, most of the patients who come to the clinic are

discouraged; they are the walking wounded. I see how satisfied and happy they are after they have worked hard and completed treatment," Dr. K. announced one day to the staff. "It's due to the great work you all do here, and I want to sincerely thank you."

"No, Dr. K., it has to do mainly with your medical excellence, caring bedside manner, and treatment of patients in general," the staff readily replied. They didn't know how much that answer, would help Ben get through the lowest of times he was yet to experience.

Chapter 25

The change in our lives came in like a hurricane, one perfectly calm and normal day, and blew us away. It left a path of destruction that could never be rebuilt. It tore up years of a career. The damage it did was irreparable.

The deluge started the day the mailman rang the doorbell with a letter that needed a signature. After receiving and reading it, I hesitated giving it to Ben for fear of his reaction. The letter was from the Board of Medical Practice in and for the state of Delaware. It was a complaint alleging that Dr. K., licensed to practice medicine in the state of Delaware, violated several sections of the Delaware codes and had to appear before the Board of Medicine. My hand was shaking as I read it, and by the time I called out to Ben, I was crying. The letter seemed so ominous and accusing. The terms used to describe the violations were horrible allegations.

"What the hell is this? They can't be serious. I've never subscribed to any of what is being said in this letter," he contended. "How could there possibly be this complaint against me? And, wait a minute, this complaint stems from a review of my records from five years ago. It's taken the board five years to decide to file this complaint? This is crazy. What do I do now?"

"Well, I think the first thing we should do is call an attorney. We should also call our insurance company to see if we are covered for the costs of litigation, because my guess is we will need it," I cautioned.

We quickly found out our insurance did not cover administrative costs and we were on our own. After making several inquiries, we found a healthcare attorney who had us fax the letter to him, and since it was already Friday afternoon, we were told he would review it on Monday. We had the entire weekend to worry and fret about the news we had just received. The letter used terms such as unprofessional conduct, unethical conduct, and negligence. If the goal of this letter was to intimidate, it was succeeding, and we spent two days very anxious and upset.

Monday morning came with a call from the attorney, telling us this was serious, but assuring us we would disagree with and argue these accusations to clear up the matter. We were at a complete loss as to why it took five years for this to appear. I had just read that Delaware had been ranked at the bottom of all the states in number of doctors disciplined. So, it couldn't be that the board was so overwhelmed and busy with its caseload, which kept it from getting to this one. Maybe the board felt obligated to come up with a disciplinary case to change Delaware's ranking. After all, Ben was already out of state, so no one would have to confront him on a daily basis. Something just wasn't right, and it made me even more nervous.

We didn't know where to begin. The practice had been sold and all the charts went to that doctor. After five years, who knew where those charts might be. The letter referenced twenty-three charts from a six month time period that had been reviewed. During that period of review, several thousand patients had been seen. It was getting strange.

We had a conference with our attorney in which he made a plan to move forward to answer the complaint. He was to call the board and request the original complaint and check on the availability of getting copies of the records in question.

A week went by before the attorney finally called us.

"The records will be available for you to see and review at the office of the board. You should do that first to make sure the complete records are there and nothing is missing," he said. "In addition, for your info, my fee is two hundred dollars per hour."

The day Ben and I chose to travel to Delaware was difficult for us. We were apprehensive but confident that the medical records we had to review would be just fine.

The twenty-three records were piled on a long table in a conference room, and as soon as we arrived, we got to the task of going through them and taking notes. Much to our chagrin, what we feared might be true, was true. Parts of several of the records were missing. It stands to reason that over a five-year period that might happen. After all, the records had been in another physician's office for all that time. What we did recognize, immediately, was that the twenty-three records were for twenty-three patients who had chronic conditions. They would naturally be those patients who had the most tests done. These charts stood out of the more than two thousand patients, seen in a time period of six months, where the reviewer was looking for extra testing. So, we were not surprised to see the charts of those patients Ben recognized as definitely being his more chronic patients.

With those patients, he always added a short narrative on the jacket cover of the record, as a reference of explanation, for any repeat tests he might have to do. This was designed to make it easier for the doctor or the nurse to quickly identify those patients, without having to dig through the entire record to try to find the diagnosis. It was a great system and worked for more than twenty-five years. To our horror, however, all the jacket covers had been replaced by the doctor who had purchased the practice. This would have been normal for the new office to do.

So we had to start digging through all the records. Three hours later, we had seen all the notes and made comments on everything in a notebook. The entries in the records mostly seemed in order, although there were several physical examination notes in some patients' records that were missing. But we felt confident that once Ben could explain this to the board, all would be well. We were also very naïve.

Armed with our notes, we contacted our attorney and mailed him all the information. Two weeks later he informed us that a hearing would be scheduled, and we would have to be lining up expert witnesses to testify on Dr. K.'s behalf. Witnesses for both sides would have to have depositions first. This was all new and frightening for us. We had never had to deal with anything like this before and the process seemed overwhelming.

The first person we decided to have testify was Dina, the nurse who assisted Ben for the last five years of his practicing in Delaware. She was well aware of the kind of convictions he had. She was in disbelief when we contacted her with the news of the complaint. She also noted that the complaint was brought about by the doctor that Ben had complained about to his group and the patient that we had taken to court for nonpayment. On the board was the surgeon that Ben had chastised about how one of his patients was treated.

"I will do whatever I can to make sure the board understands how Dr. K. practices and that our office did everything correctly," she assured us.

We then located Dr. Frank, a respected, Board Certified cardiologist in Philadelphia, whom Ben had referred his chronic heart patients to. He voiced his support and agreed to review the charts which pertained to heart patients and to also testify to the correctness of electrocardiogram testing and spirometry testing.

There was also a local Board Certified internal medicine physician, whom Ben referred his patients to, who also agreed to review records and help in any way he could concerning anoscopy and sigmoidoscopy tests.

It took months and months of letters, phone calls, and depositions till at last came that fateful day in 1990 when we appeared for the beginning of the hearing. It felt less like a hearing and more like a trial. Even at that juncture, we could not fully comprehend the intensity of what was about to occur.

Chapter 26

The room where the hearing was to take place was small, cold, and austere. Everyone involved took their seats on straight wooden chairs. My eyes scanned the room, noting that everyone appeared very rigid and tense. It might well have been a hearing for a murder trial. The mood was very serious. In glancing around the room, my eyes stayed on the doctor who had instigated the investigation and on the highly polished, black leather, knee-high boots he was wearing. His khaki pants were tucked inside those boots like riding pants, and I was wondering where his suit was—all the other men were wearing suits. He was shaking his pen back and forth in his hand like a riding crop, till he placed it down on the table with force.

As I focused on his boots I had a flashback to an SS officer, wearing black leather boots, sitting indifferently and staring at me. I think my heart stopped beating for a few seconds as I blinked the image away. Now, the doctor was staring at me. I felt my blood run cold. I had a strange déjà vu moment as scenes of a trial were taking place in an antiquated courtroom with that same SS officer. I shuddered. Returning to reality, I wiped the tears which had formed in the corners of my eyes and tried to be calm. The doctor was still staring at me.

The members of the medical board sat facing us at a dark mahogany table, and a transcriptionist sat near one end at a separate table. The witness chair was at the other end of the same table. This was a hearing but it had a courtroom feeling. The attorneys and the opposition witnesses sat at a small table to our side, facing the board members, and our lawyers and witnesses sat with us at a table also facing the board. It seemed unusual, but the board's attorney was also acting in the capacity of judge, and we were told that he would be making decisions on what would be allowed or disallowed at the hearing. We were also told that the opening statements would be made by the board first, and then our opening statements would follow. The games had begun!

The opening statements, by the board's attorney, were fairly short and direct. They did however describe a doctor who was unrecognizable to me. Surely they weren't talking about Dr. K. Our attorney gave a more lengthy opening and after listening to him, I was feeling a certain degree of confidence. Right at the beginning, he chastised the board for even pursuing these allegations and, with a great deal of passion, even requested a dismissal of the case.

"Are you serious? The fact that these proceedings have even gone to this level is a travesty of justice. I would like to make a motion for dismissal of this entire misdirected case. I think this whole thing is a kangaroo court and another example of good ol' boys justice!" our lawyer said in a very loud voice.

But the board, of course, disagreed and ordered the hearing to go forward.

The questions and answers by all the attorneys involved seemed to go on forever. After the opening statements, the board's two witnesses explained the charges and were questioned separately by the attorney. I could not believe it when their witness, a hospital based physician, testified that the spirometry test was not necessary. A patient's breathing could be measured by having him blow out a match. Ben and I just looked at each other in amazement. Then our attorney asked each witness questions, paving the way for our first witness to begin to defend the accusations.

The testimony of Dr. Frank, the Philadelphia cardiologist, had been videotaped in Philadelphia due to his busy schedule. It was played that day, in its entirety for the board to view. The questioning was laborious. To my horror, one of the board members had nodded off shortly after Dr. Frank began and kept falling asleep on and off during the testimony. So, it appeared that member only heard a partial account of our witness and would have no clue of the important things he said. I was upset that the board member was asleep when the board's attorney made a point favorable to Dr. K.'s case when he asked Dr. Frank the following question:

"And would you agree with me that there are, at least with respect to some views of level of care and what should be done in levels of care, variations when one considers the fact of Hahnemann Hospital and where it is and say, Milford Hospital in Delaware, or a family practitioner in Milford, Delaware?"

"Yes."

"OK. In other words, what might be considered as generally

accepted good practice in Philadelphia may be considered as a bit excessive or different than what might be accepted in Milford?"

"It might. I would hope it would not."

The questioning of Dr. Frank proceeded on the videotape.

At that point, it was noted that the twenty-three charts discredited by the board were reduced to seven. Again, these were seven of the most chronic patients in Dr. K.'s practice. Three of the seven were actually referred to, and seen by, Dr. Frank in consultation.

Each patient record was reviewed by our attorney with Dr. Frank. It was a two-hour process. The same questions were asked of the doctor after each review.

"Do you see the medical justification in the chart when you take the time to read it?"

"Yes."

"Do you think the tests were appropriate and not excessive?"

"Yes."

The opposing attorney opened his questioning seemingly bent on trying to show, for some reason unknown to me at the time, that Dr. Frank was a close friend of Dr. K's.

"Have you seen Dr. K. in any social function since 1986?"

"Once."

"Once, and what was that social function?"

"About three years ago, he called me and said he had moved back into the Philadelphia area. We had never met in person, so my wife and I were invited to dinner at his home."

"Did you know where he was practicing?"

"I believed it was in Delaware, and he told me it was now in Philadelphia, but I don't believe we discussed this at all. It was purely a social meeting."

"Okay, and you said you had spoken to him on at least one other occasion."

"Correct. This was about four or five weeks ago and the character of that call concerned my ability to help in this case."

"Are you being compensated for that?"

"Absolutely not."

"Okay. All right. You described Dr. K., based on your review of his files, as a very careful physician. Is that a phrase used to describe those who test more than other doctors?"

"No."

"Lastly, have you reviewed the Blue Cross billing forms?"

"I have not seen those forms, have not even seen insurance forms in my own practice."

At that point our attorney had some additional questions. He asked again about the validity of tests given on specific patients. The point was to show there were some positive findings on many of the tests.

Dr. Frank summed it up, "I had a moderate amount of contact with Dr. K., mostly with phone conversations, as I saw a number of his patients. I feel he was a very thorough doctor. When he found an abnormality, it bothered him and he wanted an answer if possible."

I glanced at Ben's face. It was serious, grim. Ben was not a person who dealt well with confrontation, and I could sense he was in pain, thinking of when he would have to be the witness.

"Are you all right?" I whispered, leaning toward him.

"Oh, I'm just dandy," he replied. "I feel like I'm about to walk a plank, and I'm getting more anxious and angry as this goes on."

My heart was breaking for him.

The next witness was Dr. Kapman, a gastroenterologist, practicing in the same town as Dr. K. had practiced in. There was testimony again that Dr. K. had been doing a thorough and conscientious job of taking care of his patients.

However, the opposing lawyer continued to try to discredit our witnesses. The best retort came from Dr. Kapman, when he was asked by the board's attorney about Blue Cross forms.

"Doctor, when you reviewed these files, did you also review the Blue Cross forms that were used to justify payments?"

"No, I have no familiarity with those types of forms. My business manager handles all those things. I wouldn't even know what one looked like."

By having worked with Ben in a medical office, I would venture to say that almost every practicing physician would have the exact same answer.

The one person who was very qualified to answer questions about Dr. K.'s patient care was his nurse, Dina. They worked closely together as a great team. The patients responded to and loved the care they received from both of them. When it came time for her to testify, I was teary-eyed.

After the swearing in of his nurse, the questions began from our attorney. He asked her questions about how Dr. K. ran his practice and what type of practice it was.

Dina described the family practice which included occupational medicine and preventive medicine.

"He didn't like to treat just symptoms. He was very much into preventive medicine and would try to get to the cause. He was very big in patient education where we would try to explain what we were doing, why we were doing it, and what the test results meant. If there was any literature that we could give them, you know, we would give it to them, and I would go over it with them, telling them if there were any questions, they could call."

She went on to explain that tests done in the office were only given if there was a reason, with most of them being given to the more chronically ill patients.

The attorney pressed on and had Dina testify about the complete physical exams done in the office, how the diagnosis on each patient was made and entered into the chart, and how that information was extracted to bill insurance companies.

Dina confirmed that neither she nor the staff ever made up a diagnosis for purposes of billing. She was also witness to the fact that the doctor always wrote his findings of diagnosis in the chart, and she would verify they were accurate, as she was very familiar with each patient.

The nurse was then asked if she had anything further to add that would assist the panel in making their decision. Her answer was special.

"I felt I learned a lot when I was working with Dr. K. I believe he truly cared for his patients. In the five years since he has been gone, I have had patients stop me on the street and ask me if I have talked to him and if he is coming back. They have made remarks that they have never had as close care and as careful supervision as they had with Dr. K.

"I think the way I can sum it up was a patient we had, a mother of seven and a cancer victim. I was called to her home in April to find out that she was dying. I had been called there, as a friend, because she wanted to tell me good-bye. One of the last things she said to me was 'Please call Dr. K. and tell him I love him.'"

Our attorney then spoke, "We have nothing further."

When I glanced back at Ben, the look of anger seemed to be gone, replaced with sadness. The opposing attorney had only a few questions for the nurse. He tried to make Dina testify that the diagnosis for testing was not always in the chart so the doctor or staff would then make one up to complete the billing. She appeared to thwart him with each question. I wondered if the members of the board were seeing through to the truth and not just seeing what their attorney tried to imply.

"Ma'am, one final question. Is it your understanding that the charts the doctors are supposed to keep should be complete?"

"Yes."

"Okay, no further questions."

I couldn't believe there were no other questions for her. It was bizarre. It felt like a trick. Ben just shook his head. The anger had returned.

Now it was my turn. After being sworn in, the direct examination began. I was asked what my occupation was and where I had been a medical office manager for twenty-five years. I was questioned about my responsibilities and the type of practice Dr. K. had. There were many questions about preventive medicine and the fact that part of my responsibilities included making sure patients received information about any test that they were about to receive.

I had to explain thirty-nine defendant exhibits of articles from *Family Practice News, Pulmonary Medicine, Cardiology Magazine,* and colon cancer studies. These were documents I had on file, and I was glad I had kept them since they became an important point of reference. I was called upon to testify on all the articles. After giving testimony on thirty-four, I was exhausted.

Our attorney explained that because of the gravity of the situation, he was requesting all these articles be reviewed to prove that the best experts in their field of medicine were advocating certain updated health management and monitoring. He had me testify at length about our successful smoking cessation program and the use of the spirometry test to monitor smokers and encourage them to quit.

I was shown a Blue Cross/Blue Shield form and testified we had never been turned down on any patient billing nor had any complaints. If our fee occasionally was higher than their prevailing fee, then we would only get paid their amount. Again, we reviewed how the diagnosis was extracted from the chart and how different tests were given to different patients when they had a complete physical examination, depending on what their complaint or findings were.

Then came my cross examination by the board's attorney.

"Are you related to Dr. K.?"

"Yes."

"How are you related?"

"I am his wife."

No further questions were asked. I thought this to be a bit bizarre and was also beginning to have an uncomfortable feeling of being set up. My take on the hearing was that the board had already passed judgment.

It was decided since the next witness would be Ben, and his testimony might be long, it would be good to call a recess. We all left the hearing room and our party walked across the street to get something to eat. Although the café we chose was quaint and very nice, Ben and I just settled for coffee. We had lost our appetite, but our attorney ordered a triple-decker deli sandwich quickly, saying he needed some fuel to keep going. Frankly, just looking at it made me nauseous. When it was time to return, I felt more nauseous.

On the walk back, Ben went on and on in a tirade.

"Why are they doing this to me? It seems they are trying to find anything they can to prove I did something wrong. If I had, in fact, been doing something they did not approve of, then why wait five years to conduct a hearing? If it was so negative, then why was the board not worried about me practicing that very medicine I believe in for those five years? This excuse of the board being so busy there was no time to get to my case is just bull. I think the board was put on the spot and had to come up with cases to raise their status. The reason Delaware was so low on the list of states reprimanding doctors was that there were so few cases. I became the sacrificial lamb and a good candidate because I am out of state. No one would have to face me. Out of the thousands of patients I saw that year, why are they so vehement about seven charts? Why, after five years, are they so interested in making a case of this?"

I couldn't answer. Ben was over-the-edge upset. My heart ached for him.

Chapter 27

When everyone was settled back in the hearing room, Ben was sworn in and direct examination began by our attorney. He testified that he had been a physician for thirty-one years and special attention was given to his decision when to relocate to Philadelphia. The "when" was really important because the opposing attorney had intimated that, when a board member told Ben a complaint had been made, he had moved to Philadelphia the very next week. Ridiculous! He had already made plans months before to sell his practice to a local physician who kindly saw his patients when we were on vacation. Six months prior, he had negotiated a contract for his practice with his new partner.

All of the patients' records were gone over with a fine-tooth comb, and Dr. K. explained every test and every diagnosis. However, because all of these patients had been chronically ill patients, the diagnoses and other pertinent information were recorded on the inside front covers of the charts, as well as in the doctor's notes. This made them immediately available, and the doctor or nurse would not have to rummage through the entire chart to find out what a true diagnosis might be. As luck would have it, when the medical practice was sold, the new doctor replaced all the covers and disposed of the old ones. With the old ones went the diagnosis of those patients, and more importantly, the reasons for some of the repeat tests that were done.

At issue was one chart in particular. It was the chart of a young man, a state trooper, who had been diagnosed with AIDS. Dr. K., wanting to preserve the patient's privacy, had used a type of code, on the inside cover of his chart, to identify the diagnosis. It was in the day when a patient might lose a job if it were known that AIDS was a diagnosis. The code was known to the nurse as well, but unfortunately, never seen by the hearing panel, leading them to assert that some tests completed on this patient were not medically indicated in the patient's file. If the chart had been reviewed five years prior, no problem.

Our attorney asked one last question, "Did you ever order any test on a patient for monetary gain?"

"No, never," Ben replied with exasperation.

The opposing attorney then seemed to be on a track to discredit Dr. K.'s entire philosophy of medicine. Even though our witnesses gave excellent opinions as to the necessity of tests ordered, it was suggested by the opposing attorney that the only reasons for these tests were financial gain.

The more aggressive the attorney was in his questioning, the more agitated Ben became. Ben was stressed to the max. I could see he was literally shaking with rage.

At one point Ben looked at him and said, "Why are you doing this to me?"

The attorney just glared at him with a smug look.

We had the opportunity to hear all kinds of assumptions. One was that we gave out information pamphlets to our patients so they would insist on having more testing. This was crazy and so wrong. Dr. K. had given out information pamphlets during and after his Air Force days. Another was that I was the doctor's wife, so I would naturally be prone not to tell the truth. Yet another one was that Dr. Frank was a friend of Ben's and would lie to support him. Insane!

As I listened to the entire hearing, I became convinced that Delaware medicine was, indeed, about five years behind medicine being practiced in Philadelphia. There definitely was a difference in the philosophy of the Philadelphia doctor who reviewed Dr. K.'s charts and the doctor who reviewed for the board. The board's reviewer was a former board member, and certainly they could not discredit him by voting for Dr. K. They couldn't even find fault when that doctor wrote in his report that "patients did not need to have a spirometry to measure breathing, they could just blow out a match." Unbelievable! The same doctor who reviewed the charts gave his opinion and then gave his statement on what the discipline for Dr. K. should be. His review was supposed to be objective, and he had no right to assume Dr. K. was censorable much less suggest any disciplinary action. This was the same doctor who lost out on a contract awarded to Dr. K.

It would play out in the history of medicine that preventive care presented a new wave of medical thinking and was essential in insuring a person's wellness. Insurance companies embraced the concept because ultimately it would save money. I guess Dr. K. may have been just a little ahead of the curve and perhaps slightly ahead of his time. But in 1991, the board seemed determined to discredit anything new, or traditionally different, when they heard this case. In hindsight, I believe the outcome had already been decided long before this hearing took place.

The summary by each attorney was next on the agenda. The board's attorney painted a picture of a doctor who performed certain tests that were not medically indicated. The reason given was for financial gain.

Our attorney pointed out that, to try and prove their point, the board presented two witnesses who were not general medicine or family practice doctors. One was a doctor, who had not practiced general medicine for thirteen years and whose practice methods were antiquated.

The other was a hospital-based physician who had not treated a patient in a family practice ever, but had testified that he did not feel the tests were medically necessary.

Our attorney jumped on the allegation that Dr. K. was only interested in financial gain and pointed out that the sum of all these tests amounted to less than nine hundred dollars.

Proceeding further, our attorney addressed the five-year delay, and the fact that due process was ignored. Dr. K. was denied the right of production of complaint documents, the right to depositions, and the right to answers to interrogatories. He pointed out that the patients' files had parts missing and, had five years not passed, some issues could have readily been resolved.

The opposing attorney suggested that Dr. K.'s patients were primed to love being overtested.

Our attorney's retort was well-stated. "I am going to submit to this panel that I don't know anybody who likes subjecting himself to an anoscopy, which is a rectal exam. It is an intrusive test and is not something that somebody runs back to the doctor for. It is not something that the doctor is thrilled about doing. The fact of the matter is, good medicine dictated that he do those tests."

A review was made of our witnesses and the qualifications and knowledge they brought to the hearing. Their expert testimony, in support of the testing done on all seven patients, surely could not have been any better for Dr. K.

The hearing ended, and people filed out of that little room. The board would reconvene in about a week to decide and judge. We were so happy and relieved to get out of there, but feeling anxious and very impatient about waiting for the board's determination. This would be the longest week of our lives.

Chapter 28

The trip home was long and quiet. Both Ben and I were mulling over the events of the hearing in our minds, and in our disbelief, we had both chosen to be silent, alone with our thoughts. We were both in shock that a seemingly small matter had been turned around to look like a big problem. Once we safely returned to our own home, the dam burst, and it became a matter of who would talk first and unload feelings.

"This is like a nightmare. I can't fathom what's just happened. The whole thing has been blown way out of proportion, and it seems that I have no control of the situation. I feel I have absolutely done nothing wrong. I don't know where these people are coming from," Ben said, with a great deal of emotion and tears forming in his eyes.

He was sad. I was angry.

"Those bastards seemed absolutely pleased to do what they are doing. It's as if they are hell-bent on winning, not because it's right or just, but because they are desperate for a win. The board appears to have a need to sanction someone, to show they are doing their job," I answered.

Since it was Friday and the end of the workweek, we, at least, had the weekend to try and relax. We were distressed, but not depressed because we truthfully felt a bit upbeat about the outcome of the hearing. We were optimistic that our witnesses' testimonies would show the board that the tests done for Dr. K.'s patients were appropriate and medically necessary.

Before we knew it, another workweek had arrived, and Ben was back in his clinic doing what he liked best. It was good that he was busy. By contrast, I was home reviewing the hearing over and over again in my mind, till I thought I would lose it. Would this week never end? Midweek we received a call summoning us back to hear the board's decision, so on Friday we found ourselves and our attorney once again in defensive mode, sitting and waiting for someone from the board to speak.

We were surprised to find out that the board would actually be voting while we were present, and there would have to be a majority vote either way for an outcome. We anxiously watched it all play out. The board's president called for a vote and each member was asked to raise his hand for a yea or nay vote to sanction. We were stunned to lose our case by a count of four to one! The board explained how they reached that vote. Before we had all assembled, they had met and decided to discount all our expert witness testimony because the witnesses had not seen the Blue Cross/ Blue Shield bills. That was it!

Afterward, they formally issued a reprimand to Dr. K. in a five-minute discourse and advised him that he would receive a written reprimand in the near future. Disbelief showed on Ben's face as the decision was read, and he kept shaking his head in nonacceptance. There followed about ten minutes of legal jargon from both sides, and we were then dismissed. No one at our table could move.

We sat frozen in time till our attorney announced, "Don't worry. We are going to appeal. Let's go."

We left the hearing like zombies and were happy that our attorney had elected to drive, because neither of us was able to get behind the wheel of a car. We felt used and abused, with Ben getting the impression that he was like a pawn in a chess game, and he never had a chance to win.

"This is so wrong," Ben kept mumbling under his breath all the way home. "Why would the board not want to see the truth?"

I felt I had been right all along. The decision we heard that day was made long before the hearing, influenced possibly by the board's reviewer, who had suggested a sanction before any evidence had ever been heard.

When the shock wore off, we busied ourselves with everyday life, but the cloud of that outcome hung over us and shut out much of the sun. Ben was downtrodden and disappointed. Our family and close friends were aware of what happened and were alarmed and worried about the stress he was under.

Being the eternal optimist, however, I tried to put things in perspective.

"Listen, Ben, it was only a reprimand. You are still practicing medicine and can continue to do things you consider important. Most of all, you have a clear conscience and have done no harm. Your intent is good and your patients love you. You're a super doctor. That's what really counts."

I actually got a smile from him after that little speech.

Months went by and an appeal was filed in the Superior Court of the State of Delaware, which we lost. It was ruled that the law was followed and nothing was improper.

We then filed further in the Supreme Court of the State of Delaware and again lost. The judge ruled the law had been followed, but also stated that he found the way the case had been handled was deplorable. But, of course, that did not do us one bit of good. We were forced to accept what had happened. Ben did write a letter to the board, however, to let them know his opinion:

To Members of the Board,

I am writing this letter after appeals were made trying to reverse the outcome of my hearing in 1991. Unfortunately, appeals can only be heard on matters of law and although the Supreme Court of Delaware said that the way my case was handled was "deplorable," it was within the law.

At this time I would like to go on record as saying that the hearing panel's findings are a set of completely false conclusions. I have practiced medicine for over three decades and have never made up a diagnosis for the purpose of billing, nor has any of my office staff. I am a person with ethics. I have practiced and continue to practice quality medicine, doing tests I believe in, while giving the best care I can to my patients. I have been commended by my colleagues for my excellent work-ups and my ability to keep patients out of the hospital. In all these years, I have had no malpractice cases or insurance complaints. I can verify that my records can stand up to any physician's because I do record review for several companies and have access to many medical records. I did not deserve a reprimand by the board as I have done nothing wrong.

I feel the entire hearing was a farce, including the fact that one of the hearing panel members fell asleep during my witness, Dr. Frank's, testimony. Dr. Frank is a highly credentialed physician who reviewed my records and found all the tests I did to be medically necessary. Imagine, the panel discounted his testimony because he did not see insurance bills.

I believe I was targeted because of political pressure put on the board after a poll of medical boards was published, and Delaware was rated very low for doctor discipline. Also, I no longer practiced in Delaware, so I was a perfect candidate for this action; no one had to face me in the community.

The truth will win only if you continue to speak it over and over again. I again reiterate to the board: I have never done a test on a patient that was not within accepted standard of care for that patient's benefit. I feel I am innocent of the issues I was reprimanded for. Since legislative law has allowed this to happen, I will be writing and talking to anyone who will listen who can possibly implement change, so that a murderer in the state of Delaware does not have more rights than a physician.

Even in bad times, there are sometimes joyful events that help balance life out. After the hearing, our married son Scott had a son. Then Michael was married. Soon after, David graduated college. Then Scott had a daughter. Things were once again on track. Ben was totally back in the swing of things in his practice, even with all the challenges and changes. I still worked in the office and enjoyed the day-to-day contact with the patients. Life seemed good again.

Of course, we both worked hard at making life seem like it was good. In actuality, there was always an undercurrent of negative feelings, stemming from his sanction, which kept eating at him.

"You know I feel so demoralized. I've lost some self confidence in my decision making when it comes to my patients," Ben said one morning as we finished our breakfast. "I stand firm in my beliefs about testing and preventive care, but I also feel beaten down. It's not that I'm not a good doctor; it's just that I'm so hard on myself. I question every little thing, wondering if some record reviewer would approve. It used to be that a doctor's notes were notations to himself of patients' problems and progress. It's just not that way anymore."

I looked at him across the table and felt so bad. He looked older and painfully stressed out. That sparkle in his persona had all but disappeared.

"Listen," I explained (as if I really had to tell him), "medicine is progressing so fast, and new medical discoveries are taking place even as we speak. Medical philosophy changes every year, mostly according to the latest studies being done. Surely, they will prove that catching disease before it becomes a problem is the best and even the cheapest way to go."

"You're right, someday preventive health care will be totally accepted, and the medical world will have to pay attention," he responded, as he hastily slipped out the door on the way to the office.

"And maybe, then, you'll feel vindicated," I shouted after him. But he had already closed the door and probably didn't hear me. In my heart, I hoped what I said would be true.

Chapter 29

I guess I am only fooling myself, if I say that I don't know what ultimately killed him. I saw it coming and fault myself for not taking the matter more seriously. He had actually preached to me for years about the role stress played in people's lives, and how he believed it was responsible for most medical problems. He even went out on a limb many times, saying to me, "You know almost half of the patients whom I care for have problems directly related to stress." How prophetic.

He had never had a heart problem, so the idea of his dying of a heart attack at such a comparatively early age did not even cross my mind. It was a peaceful death and I am grateful for that.

We had just finished dinner and, as was pretty much routine in our house, I awaited the accolades. There were a few times when they were not forthcoming, but it had to be a pretty bad meal for that to happen.

"The eggplant was simply delicious. You know exactly how I like it made," he said. "I think I'll catch the news on television in the den."

He seemed so calm and peaceful, more so than he had been for months. It gave me a sense of hope that we could put all the bad behind us.

"I'll be right there. Glad you liked the eggplant. Love you," I shouted to him, as he walked down the hall.

I wish I had left those dirty dishes in the sink. I wish I had not stopped to clean off the kitchen counters. I wish I had walked into the den sooner. I knew CPR. I could have done something. By the time I entered the den and realized he was not answering me when I was talking to him, and by the time I figured out he was not asleep, it was too late. He was lifeless! He was gone! I quickly called 911 and did try CPR, but to no avail. I just held him tight.

I unlocked the door for the medics and went back to cradling Ben in my arms. I rocked him gently as if it would somehow comfort him. There were no tears. I couldn't cry. I just felt hysterical inside, with no way for the hysteria to come out. I was probably in shock. The medics had arrived within minutes, and now they pronounced him dead. After a slew of questions, I followed the ambulance to the hospital where a physician would need to further pronounce him dead and fill out a death certificate with cause of death. The cause was listed as possible heart attack. It should have been listed as "heart attack due to stress."

When I saw our three boys walk into the hospital and reality set in, my body totally fell into a helpless heap. The violent shakes came first, like a personal earthquake, which triggered an avalanche of tears. My emotions were crumbling as I fought to keep my composure. I lost the fight. The boys, sheltering me with their arms, took me home. They stayed with me throughout the night while I wailed and whimpered looking at the empty side of our bed, realizing that my life would never be the same. I felt overwhelming sadness for myself and for Ben too.

I remembered what he had recently said: "I have so much more to accomplish. The challenges in medicine are still exciting to me, and I want to do more in my lifetime to give my patients comfort and to alleviate their pain."

Those ongoing challenges were never to be fulfilled. Standing at his gravesite, in my grief, I realized it was ironic that the medicine he loved so much, the profession that he took great pride in, the career of caring that he chose so many years ago wound up killing him.

About the Author

Barbara Kotler was born in Brooklyn, New York. She moved to New Jersey with her parents at an early age, where she attended New Jersey public schools. After receiving a Bachelor of Arts degree in Elementary Education at Kean College, Barbara taught first grade till she met and married Dr. Barry Kotler, her present husband of fifty five years. They have three sons and eight grandchildren. When her husband opened his first medical practice she happily went to work in his office as his office manager, for thirty-four years.

What Killed Doctor K.? reflects an insider's candid observance of the medical world from the 60's through the 90's.

These were the years of major changes in medicine, some of which depicted conflicting times.

Although she always loved to write, her writing was limited to college essays, short stories, and articles in newsletters. Since retiring to Florida in 1999 and joining The Writers Colony of The Delray Center Of The Arts, Barbara has been writing non-stop. She is active in this group by moderating monthly "open readings" and establishing "Writers On The Go," where she and other members participate in community programs.

She is now working on her second book, *Dear Grandchildren.*

CPSIA information can be obtained at www.ICGtesting.com
Printed in the USA
LVOW07s0609020715

444589LV00002B/3/P

9 780990 887102